KU-469-728

Flirting with Italian

Liz Fielding

MILLS & BOON

DID YOU PURCHASE THIS BOOK WITHOUT A COVER?

If you did, you should be aware it is **stolen property** as it was reported *unsold and destroyed* by a retailer. Neither the author nor the publisher has received any payment for this book.

All the characters in this book have no existence outside the imagination of the author, and have no relation whatsoever to anyone bearing the same name or names. They are not even distantly inspired by any individual known or unknown to the author, and all the incidents are pure invention.

All Rights Reserved including the right of reproduction in whole or in part in any form. This edition is published by arrangement with Harlequin Enterprises II BV/S.à.r.l. The text of this publication or any part thereof may not be reproduced or transmitted in any form or by any means, electronic or mechanical, including photocopying, recording, storage in an information retrieval system, or otherwise, without the written permission of the publisher.

This book is sold subject to the condition that it shall not, by way of trade or otherwise, be lent, resold, hired out or otherwise circulated without the prior consent of the publisher in any form of binding or cover other than that in which it is published and without a similar condition including this condition being imposed on the subsequent purchaser.

® and TM are trademarks owned and used by the trademark owner and/or its licensee. Trademarks marked with ® are registered with the United Kingdom Patent Office and/or the Office for Harmonisation in the Internal Market and in other countries.

First published in Great Britain 2011
by Mills & Boon, an imprint of Harlequin (UK) Limited,
Eton House, 18-24 Paradise Road, Richmond, Surrey TW9 1SR

© Liz Fielding 2011

ISBN: 978 0 263 88516 3

Harlequin (UK) policy is to use papers that are natural, renewable and recyclable products and made from wood grown in sustainable forests. The logging and manufacturing process conform to the legal environmental regulations of the country of origin.

Printed and bound in Spain
by Blackprint CPI, Barcelona

Also by Liz Fielding

Mistletoe and the Lost Stiletto
SOS: Convenient Husband Required
A Wedding at Leopard Tree Lodge
Her Desert Dream
Secret Baby, Surprise Parents
Wedded in a Whirlwind

Did you know these are also available as eBooks?
Visit www.millsandboon.co.uk

™

I dedicate this book to my wonderful editor, Bryony Green, who has held my hand, uncomplainingly, through more than twenty books. She has saved a book gone wrong with 'Perhaps if you…' We have agonised over titles, dined in New York, celebrated an award at the Ritz and danced the night away in Washington. It's been great.

TM

CHAPTER ONE

ITALIAN FOR BEGINNERS

My bag is packed, my flight booked. While my students are all flapping about in a last minute panic about coursework that needs to be handed to their new teacher in the first week of term, I'll be getting to grips with the rush hour in Rome, first day nerves and life in a foreign language.

If they think that because I'll be surrounded by art, culture, high fashion and endless sunshine, I've got the best deal, well, they may be right. At the moment I'm only concerned about where I'm going to live, how different this new school will be from Maybridge and whether my new students like me.

Watch this space...

'I've got a new job, Lex. In Rome.'

'You're leaving Maybridge High? The "world's most perfect job"?'

Sarah Gratton had been doing a fine job of convincing her colleagues that she couldn't wait to get on that plane. Actually, that part was true, but it was more escape than adventure and she should have known that her great-grandfather would see right through a smile that was making her face ache.

He might be rising ninety but he walked into town each morning to pick up his newspaper, and his brain was still sharp enough to do *The Times* crossword in ten minutes flat.

'Tom was so popular, the kids loved him.' Her thumb automatically moved to fiddle with the ring that was no longer there. 'I feel as if everyone blames me for him leaving.'

'He's the one who cheated, Sarah. If you give up the job you love, you lose twice.'

'He didn't cheat.'

Didn't cheat. Didn't lie. Didn't pretend. He was incapable of that. He'd told her that he still loved her, but that he'd fallen in love with someone else.

He'd told her at the beginning of the half term holiday, giving her a whole week before she had to walk into the staff room. Face everyone.

What he hadn't told her was that he'd resigned, taken a job she knew he'd hate at the sports centre in Melchester.

Until then it hadn't been real.

She'd heard the words but hadn't been able to take them in. Had convinced herself that when she turned up in the staffroom on Monday morning everything would be as it should be. Back to normal.

But he hadn't been there.

He'd had time to think it through, to accept that working together in the goldfish bowl of school would be impossible. He was the one who'd sacrificed the job that was his life. That was how much he loved her.

How much he was *in love* with someone else.

She'd worked really hard to be worthy of that sacrifice. To think of her students when all she wanted to do was to curl up in a corner and bawl her eyes out.

She'd cleaned every trace of him out of her flat so that she wouldn't keep tripping over the memories. Put away photographs. Stopped going to the places where they'd hung out with their friends.

But she couldn't scrub him out of school.

He was an invisible presence in the photographs of the teams he'd coached to glory. In the whiff of steaming boys, the clatter of their boots as they came in from the cricket field. In the sound of a whistle on the sports field that had once linked her to him like an invisible thread, but now went through her like a knife.

'Besides,' she said, 'I'm not losing, I'm catching up on my life. You were the one who was so keen on me taking a gap year, having fun, doing the travel thing before I settled down.'

'You're not eighteen now,' her great-grandfather pointed out. 'And you're not taking a year off to see the world or have fun.'

'I'd feel like a matron amongst the backpackers. This way I get the best of both worlds. Great job. Great location. I only hope I live up to the terrific reference the Head gave me.'

He dismissed her doubts with a wave of his hand. 'Won't the language be a problem?'

'It's an international school. Children of diplomats, UN officials, foreigners living in Rome,' she explained.

Eight hundred miles away from everyone who knew her as half of a couple.

It had been Tom-and-Sarah from the first day she'd started at Maybridge High when, shaking with nerves, she'd managed to throw a cup of coffee over the blond giant who was head of the sports department. Instead of calling her the idiot she clearly was, he'd smiled, and in the gaze of his clear blue eyes the world had steadied.

She'd offered to wash his kit. He'd said he'd settle for a pint, and her world had remained steady until a new supply teacher had arrived one dark morning in January when half the staff were laid low with flu.

It had been like watching an approaching car crash that she was powerless to stop. The sudden silence as a new face had appeared in the staffroom. Tom, the first to step forward to welcome her—always, always so kind with new people. The contact had lasted no more than a second or two but time had seemed to stand still as their eyes met and, as Sarah looked on, she'd felt the scorching heat of the spark that leapt between Tom and Louise, and her world had shifted off its axis.

'I'll soon get to know people,' she said. 'Teaching isn't a job you can do in isolation. And I'll be in *Rome*,' she stressed. 'One of the most glamorous cities in the world.'

In one bound she'd freed herself from being the most pitied woman in the staffroom and become the most envied.

Not that she'd escaped entirely. She'd done her best to resist the Head's suggestion that she write a blog about her experiences.

'I know it's been a tough few months, but things will look different after a break. I expect you back next year,' he'd told her.

'You don't need me, Headmaster, you need Tom. Call him.'

'And have everyone think I've got you out of the way so that I can bring him back? How would that look?' he'd asked.

Dodgy, obviously, she thought, as the penny

had dropped. That was why he wanted her to write the blog. So that it would look as if she was still part of the school.

Glowing references had, it seemed, to be paid for. And it wasn't as if anyone would read it. The staff would be too busy and, as for the kids, well, why would they bother?

Sarah started as Lex took her hand.

'It's not far,' she told him. 'I'll be home for visits so often you'll be sick of me. Half term. The holidays.'

'What for? To see an old man?' His gesture was dismissive. 'Don't waste your time or your money. Enjoy Italy while you have the chance.'

'I'll have plenty of time to see everything.' And she could travel with the money she'd been saving for her wedding, for the big dress. Her share of the deposit they had been saving for a house. One with a garden for the children they would have had one day.

'There's never enough time,' he warned her. 'Your life goes by in a flash. Enjoy every minute of it.'

'Of course,' she said, on automatic.

'No, I mean *really* enjoy it.' He regarded her with that thoughtful gaze that his patients would have recognised when he had still been in practice. The one that saw through the 'headaches' to the real problem. 'I prescribe an affair,' he said. 'No falling in love, breaking your heart stuff, mind. Nothing serious,' he warned. 'A just-for-fun romance with some dark-eyed Italian. A memory to make you smile rather than weep. To keep you warm at night when you're old.'

'Lex! You are outrageous.'

He grinned. 'Trust me. I'm a doctor.'

She laughed. 'Outrageous and wonderful and I love you.' They'd always been close. Her parents loved her, did all the parent stuff brilliantly. Her grandparents had spoiled her. But Lex was the one who never had anything better to do than tell her stories and, as he leaned back in his chair, his eyes on some unseen horizon, she knew exactly what he was going to say next.

'Did I ever tell you about the time I was in Italy during the war?'

'Once or twice.' It had been a favourite story when she was a little girl.

How his plane had developed engine trouble and he'd had to bail out. How he'd nearly died of the cold.

It was a story that had grown with the years. With the telling. Embellished, embroidered. She'd never known her great-grandmother, but her grandmother had always claimed that he never spoiled a good story by telling the truth. Her mother had simply rolled her eyes.

'Tell me again,' Sarah urged him. 'Tell me how you were saved by a beautiful Italian girl who found you half-dead in the snow. How she nursed you, hid you for months until the Allies arrived.'

'You know it by heart.'

Maybe she did, but that was the point of a comfort story. Its familiarity.

'Gran always said you made up most of it. That the lovely Lucia was really some tough old bird who hid you in her cow shed for a week,' she said, knowing exactly how to get him going. And off her case.

'Your grandmother knows nothing.' Nearly ninety but still with a wicked twinkle in his eye. 'The house had been grand before the Fascists reduced it to rubble. And Lucia was…' He stopped. 'Pass me my box and I'll show you.'

'Show me?'

There was always some new little twist to the story, some detail to be added: a new danger, a risk taken for food or warmth, a small pleasure to be found amongst the hardship. But this was totally unexpected.

'The box,' he repeated.

She'd seen the contents of the old tartan biscuit box a hundred times. There had never been a photograph of Lucia and, as she handed it to him, she half expected it to be a joke of some kind. But there was none of the usual teasing and when he opened the lid, instead of going through it—a memory recalled with each medal, photograph, memento collected during a long life, well-lived—he tipped it up, emptying everything on to the table beside him.

It was a small table and papers, coins, trinkets spilled over onto the floor. Sarah knelt to gather them up. Smoothed out the corner of the small sepia photograph of her great-grandma that he had carried with him through the war.

'Leave those,' he said. 'Your nails are longer than mine. See if you can get this out.'

The base of the box was lined with a piece of black card, scuffed by years of wear. Now, as she eased it out, she discovered that it concealed a photograph.

He gave an awkward little shrug.

'Not something to leave lying around where it would upset your great-grandmother.'

Upset?

It was an old grainy black-and-white photograph of a slender young woman with dark hair, dark eyes, dark brows, a full, sensuous mouth.

Scratched, carefully stuck together where it had obviously been torn into pieces—presumably by a very upset great-grandma—spotted with age, her face leapt out of the past.

'She was lovely,' she said, turning to catch a look of such tenderness in his eyes that she felt a lump rise to her throat. 'I can't begin to imagine how hard it must have been.'

It made her emotional hiccup seem pretty feeble in comparison.

'Be glad of that,' he told her, then seemed to drift for a moment, no doubt recalling the hardships. Or maybe it was Lucia's beauty that he remembered.

She was sitting on a crumbling stone wall, her dark hair gleaming in the sun. Behind her were the remains of a house that might well have once been grand, but was now largely rubble.

It had not, after all, been a fairy tale but real and desperate. This woman had risked her life to save a stranger, shown courage it was hard to imagine.

Her full mouth was smiling and her dark almond-shaped eyes betrayed everything she felt for the man taking the photograph. Was this a secret memory that kept him warm at night?

'I should have gone back,' he said, rousing himself. 'When it was all over. But I had a wife, a son at home...' His voice trailed away.

Sarah covered his hand with her own. 'It was wartime, Lex.' He might have been discovered at any moment. Shot. Lucia, too.

'Don't waste your time...'

'She risked her life to save me, but when the Allies reached Rome there was no time for anything. Hardly time to say goodbye before I was shipped out. Returned to a wife who had long since given me up for dead.'

'Did you ever try to get in touch?' she asked. 'After the war?'

'I wrote. Sent some money. Asked her to let me know if she needed anything. There was no reply and in the end I thought it best to let it go, thinking that letters, money from an English airman might cause her problems. Embarrassment…' He shook his head. 'Your grandmother was on the way by then, I was working night and day to catch up with my studies.' He shrugged. 'We got on with things.'

Lived with the rushed wartime marriage, vows made when his life was counted in hours rather than years.

'It was a good life,' he said, as if reading her thoughts.

'I know.' She'd turned the photograph over and read out, '"June nineteen forty-four. Isola del Serrone". Is that the village she lived in? I wonder if she's still alive?'

'She'd be in her eighties,' he said doubtfully.

'A stripling lass compared to you.' And with those bones, those eyes, she'd still be beautiful. 'You should try to find her.'

'No…'

'It shouldn't be that difficult.' She reached for his laptop and searched the internet for the name of the village. 'Let's see. An actress was

born there. And a racing driver...' She glanced
up. 'How small was this village?'

She had clicked on the link to the racing
driver and found herself looking at a photograph of a man in overalls, a crash helmet
under his arm.

'Oh, how awful!' she exclaimed.

'What?'

'The racing driver was killed in a practice
session in nineteen eighty-three, leaving a wife
and young son.' She skimmed through the cap-
tion. 'But they lived in Turin. This looks more
like it,' she said, clicking on another link. 'A
vineyard. It's a local co-operative producing
prize-winning wine...'

'Leave it, Sarah.' She looked up. 'Some things
are better left in the past.'

'Maybe.'

'Lucia will have had a family. No one wants
old skeletons to come rattling out of the cup-
board.'

'You're not an old skeleton...' Then, seeing
that he really meant it, added, 'Sorry. I'm being
bossy. It goes with the job.' But as he made a
move to return the picture to the bottom of the
box, she said, 'Don't shut her away.'

'This is in no fit state to put in a frame,' he
protested.

'I know someone who can scan it, clean it

up so that it looks like new. We all need memories to keep us warm at night. You said it,' she pointed out.

'So I did. And I'll let you take it, clean it up, if you'll promise to take the medicine I've prescribed.'

'The Italian lover?'

'Night and morning until all symptoms of heartache are completely gone,' he said with a smile.

ITALIAN FOR BEGINNERS

Oh, good grief. Where to start? Who was she talking to? Her students? Colleagues? Parents? Herself…

I can see you all, sitting on the wall before assembly, grumbling about having to read Miss Gratton's blog on top of all that revising you have to do.

You are revising? Do it right once and History will be just that. History. Unless you're living in Rome, where you're surrounded by it. No! Don't switch off!

I know you think that this blog is going to be all about ancient Romans, old ruins and churches. Boring.

That if you leave a comment I'll be marking it out of ten. Or worse, that if you don't

leave a comment telling me how much
you're missing me I'll give you cyber deten-
tion.

Who was she kidding? No fifteen-year-old
was going to waste time reading this. She was
just going through the motions. A week or two
and she could forget it. Not that the blog was
helping. It was hard not to think about Tom
back in the staffroom, his smile as he looked
up and saw her...

She sighed, reread what she'd written so far.

...cyber detention.
You can relax. I'll take it as read.
Before we get to the boring stuff...

Boring was good. The sooner they switched
off the better.

...boring stuff, however, I thought you'd
like to see where I live.
The street is very narrow, cobbled and
so steep that it has a step every couple of
metres. It's inaccessible to cars, although
that doesn't stop boys on Vespas—a danger
to life and limb—using it as a shortcut.
I live on the top floor of the yellow
house on the left. No need for a workout

*in the gym. The hill and the stairs will
keep me fit.*

It had been raining when she'd arrived and
she'd been soaked through by the time she'd
hauled her luggage up from the street. It hadn't
occurred to her to carry a raincoat; she was
going to Rome, city of eternal sunshine. Ha!

And she was out of shape. The stairs might
kill her…

*I have a tiny terrace. The geranium is a
gift from my new students (you might want
to make a note of that), who are all ex-
tremely tidy…*

More than tidy. Well groomed, fashion-con-
scious, even the boys—especially the boys—
with their designer-label wardrobes.

*…well behaved and produce their home-
work on time.*

A comment guaranteed to have her students
switching off en masse.

This is the view.

A fabulous panorama of the city. Domes, red
tiled roofs and the Victor Emmanuelle Memorial like a vast wedding cake at its heart. It was

a view made to share while you drank an early morning cup of coffee, or a glass of wine in the evening, with the city lights spread out below you.

Hard not to imagine sharing it with Tom, although he hated travelling. Getting him on the cross Channel ferry for a weekend in France had been hard work.

It was a little soon to have made any progress in the 'Italian lover' department so, for the moment, she and her mug of cocoa had it all to themselves.

You're right, there are loads of churches. The dome in the distance on the left is St Peter's, by the way. In case you're interested. And this is the Mercato Esquilino, the local market where I shop for food.

There's a lot of stuff that you won't find in Maybridge market. These zucchini flowers—courgettes to you—for instance. I bought some and put them in a bowl because the yellow is so cheery...

She deleted *cheery*. She did not want anyone to think she needed cheering up.

...so gorgeous, but the locals eat them stuffed with a dab of soft cheese and deep-fried in a feather-light batter.

And, for the girls, especially the ones in the staffroom, this is Pietro, who sells the most sublime dolcelatte and mortadella.

The food here is fabulous and I am going to need every one of those four flights of stairs if I'm not to burst out of my new clothes.

Oh, yes. The clothes.

And suddenly she was enjoying herself.

She'd been met at the airport by Pippa, the school secretary, a young Englishwoman living in Rome with her Italian boyfriend. It was Pippa who had found her the apartment on the top floor of a crumbling old house. Apparently it belonged to the boyfriend's family. Sarah's first reaction on seeing it had been, *'What?'*

It was a world away from her modern flat in Maybridge but, having been in Rome for a couple of weeks, she realised how lucky she was to get something so central. And she'd quickly fallen in love with its odd-shaped rooms, high ceilings and view.

Pippa had introduced her to the transport system, shown her around and, having taken one look at her wardrobe, warned her that the cheap and cheerful tops, skirts and trousers that had been 'teacher uniform' at Maybridge High would not cut the mustard in Rome. Here, quality, rather than quantity, mattered.

New job. New life. New clothes seemed the obvious extension and Pippa had happily introduced her to cut-price, Italian style. Discount designer outlets that specialised in Armani, Versace, Valentino. Fabulous fabrics and exquisite tailoring that looked all the better for the weight that had dropped off her in the past few months. And, of course, a pair of genuine designer sunglasses.

Her knock-offs from Maybridge market wouldn't fool anyone here, especially not her students, who wore cashmere sweaters and designer label everything with catwalk style.

Italians are incredibly elegant, even in the classroom, and my first task was a complete revamp of my working wardrobe. It was tough, but I know you'll appreciate my sacrifice.

Spending so much on clothes had come as a bit of a shock to the system but her savings account was no longer burdened with the price of her dream wedding dress. And handing over her credit card to pay for her spending spree had slammed the door on any lingering hope that Tom might come back. Or that her sacrifice in giving up her job so that he could return to Maybridge High would bring him to his senses.

It was too late for him to be having regrets.

There is also a rule that no one should come to Italy without buying at least one pair of shoes. I bought these. And these. And these.

She stretched out her foot to admire the sandal she was wearing. Well, she wasn't on holiday. One pair was never going to be enough and, just to make the point, she picked up her phone and took a photograph of it.

As you can see, there is a lot more to Rome than a load of old ruins, but since you're expecting churches and I wouldn't want to disappoint you, this is Santa Maria del Popolo. You'll probably recognise it from one of the gorier bits in the film Angels & Demons.
Rome, boring? I think not.

The blog was probably not quite what the Head had in mind, Sarah thought, smiling to herself. With luck he'd remove the link from the school website sooner rather than later. Then, as she loaded up the pictures, she wondered if Tom would bother to read it. Whether Louise could resist taking a look.

Those shoes would provoke envy in the heart of any woman. Especially one whose ankles were swelling…

Several of her ex-colleagues had made a point of texting Sarah to let her know that Louise was pregnant, but not before Tom had told her himself. Wanting her to know before she heard it from anyone else. As if it would hurt any less.

She gave herself a mental bad-girl slap as she clicked 'post', but there were limits to her nobility.

Finally, she checked her email. There was one from her mother, attaching a photograph of her dad being presented with an award from work for twenty-five years service. Another from Lex, who wanted to know how she was progressing in her search for a dark-eyed Italian lover.

Short answer; she'd had no time.

Faced with a slightly different syllabus to the one she'd been teaching, getting to know her students and finding her way around a strange city, she didn't have a spare moment. She'd even taken a rain check on Pippa's offer to go clubbing with her and her boyfriend, and she replied to Lex, telling him so.

Or perhaps she was just being cowardly. Getting back into dating was hard. She couldn't imagine being with someone else. Kissing, touching, being touched by anyone else.

There were a couple of emails from colleagues at Maybridge High, asking how she was coping. One wanting to know when she could come and stay. The other wanting to know when she'd be home for the weekend.

She wrote cheery replies saying, 'any time' to the first, 'no idea' to the second, telling them both about the shopping, sightseeing and her new colleagues, several of whom had invited her to spend her weekends with their families.

It was kind of them but the last thing she wanted was for her social life to revolve around work.

Been there. Done that. Using the T-shirt as a duster.

It wasn't as if there was any shortage of things to see and do.

Her degree might be in History but the Romans, beyond Julius Caesar, Hadrian's Wall and Antony and Cleopatra, were pretty much a blank page and her spare time had been spent being a total tourist, sucking up the sights, taking pictures.

But Lucia had been on her mind a lot and on Saturday she was going to visit the village of Isola del Serrone.

Sarah had no intention of revealing her identity. She just wanted to know what had happened to Lucia. If she had a good life. And, if she was still alive, that she was well cared for. Her family owed her that.

CHAPTER TWO

ITALIAN FOR BEGINNERS

> *This weekend, dear readers, I abandoned culture, history, the familiarity of the city and took a train ride out into the Italian countryside.*
>
> *It's a bit unnerving, buying a ticket in a foreign language. I'm working on my Italian and I can ask the right questions. 'Un'andata e ritorno, per favore…'*
>
> *Unfortunately, I don't understand the answers. It's like listening to a radio that's slipped off the station. My ear isn't tuned in to the sounds, the inflections of the language. I have to listen ten times as hard and even then I'm only catching one word in five.*
>
> *Somehow, though, I caught the right train and made it safely to my destination.*

MATTEO DI SERRONE was furious. Isabella di Serrrone might be the darling of the Italian cinema, but right at that moment she was no favourite of his.

He'd planned an early escape from Rome, but had instead become embroiled in his cousin's latest indiscretions when she'd arrived on his doorstep with an army of paparazzi in her wake.

She knew how he loathed the media. They'd all but destroyed his mother and they would do the same to her if she gave them half a chance.

Now, instead of a quiet early morning drive to Isola del Serrone, a day in the vineyards checking that everything was ready for the harvest, he was in her limousine, playing Pied Piper to her escort, with his sulky teenage brother for company.

'Cheer up, Stephano. You, at least, are getting something out of this,' Matteo said.

'Stop acting the hard man. You know you'd do anything for Bella,' came the swift reply.

He glanced at the boy. Made-up, in wig and dark glasses, with his cousin's coat thrown around his shoulders, he was pretty enough to be mistaken for her. Pretty enough to have fooled the following pack of photographers.

'Not quite anything,' Matteo said and, as he grinned, the tension leached out of him. 'I promise you that, not even for Bella, would I be prepared to wear lipstick.'

* * *

The mountains towered, clear and sharp, rising dramatically from the valley floor. Sarah looked up at them, peaceful, unthreatening in the sunlight, and tried to imagine them in the middle of winter. Covered in snow. The haunt of wolves and bears.

Unless, of course, Lex had made it up about the wolves and bears. Which was entirely possible.

Early in October, the sun was still strong enough for her to be glad of the straw hat she wore to keep it off her face. She paused by the bridge to look down at the river, trickling over stones, very low after the long hot summer. Took her time as she walked up the hill towards the village, looking around her for a glimpse of a familiar wall. The ruins of a once grand house.

Steps led up to a piazza, golden in the sunlight, shaded with trees. There were small shops, a café where the aproned proprietor was setting out tables and a church that seemed far too large for such a small place.

It was pretty enough to be a film set and she stood in the centre of the square, turning in a slow circle, taking photographs with her phone, making sure that she missed nothing.

As she came to a standstill she realised that she was being stared at by the man wearing the apron.

'*Buon giorno,*' she called.

He stared at her for a moment, then nodded briefly before retreating inside.

She shrugged. Not exactly an arms-wide welcome and, instead of crossing the square to have a coffee, ask him about the village, she walked towards the church. It was possible that the priest would be her best bet. She'd scanned a copy of Lucia's photograph onto her netbook before framing one for Lex, but she didn't have it with her. She wasn't planning on flashing it around. But she could at least describe the house.

It was dark inside after the glare of the sun, but she could see that several people were waiting in the pews by the confessional boxes. Clearly the priest was going to be busy for a while.

It was a pretty church, beautifully painted, with a number of memorial plaques on the walls. Maybe one of them would bear the name Lucia? It would be a starting place.

As she looked around, a woman arranging flowers in a niche by a statue of the Madonna stared at her over the glasses perched on the end of her nose. Clearly the village wasn't used to strangers and, feeling like an intruder, she decided to come back later when the church was quiet. Once outside, she followed a path that continued up the hill.

High ground.

That was what she needed. Somewhere she could look down on the village, see everything.

She continued upwards, passed houses tucked away behind high walls that offered only the occasional glimpse of a tiny courtyard, a pot of bright flowers, through wrought-iron gates. Above her there were trees, the promise of open vistas and she pressed on until she found the way unexpectedly blocked by a wall that looked a lot newer than the path.

There was a gate set into it but, as she reached for the handle, assuming that it was to keep goats from wandering into the village, it was flung open by a young man with a coat bundled under his arm.

It was hard to say which of them was most startled but he recovered first and, with a slightly theatrical bow, said, *'Il mio piacese, signora!'*

'No problem…' Then, as he held the gate wide for her. 'Thank you.' No… *'Grazie.'*

'My pleasure, *signora Inglese.* Have a good day,' he said, grinning broadly, clearly delighted with life.

She watched him bound down the steps. By the time he'd reached the square he was talking twenty to the dozen into his phone.

Smiling at such youthful energy, she looked around her. There was nothing beyond the wall except a rough path which led upwards through thick, scrubby woods to the top of the hill. With luck, there would be a clearing at the top, a viewpoint from which she could survey the surrounding countryside.

She closed the gate and carried on, catching the occasional glimpse of a vast vineyard sloping away into the distance on her right. Then, as she neared the top of the hill, the thicket thinned out and her heart stopped.

Ahead of her, the path edged towards a tumbledown stretch of wall. Part of it had fallen away so long ago that weeds had colonised it, growing out of cracks in the stone.

Patches of dry yellow lichens spread themselves out in the sun where Lucia had sat, smiling one last time for a man who was going away. Who she must have known she'd never see again.

Only a dusty footprint suggested that anyone had been this way since.

She took a step nearer. Reached out to lay her hand on the warm stone.

Here. Lucia had sat here. And as she looked up she saw a house. The house. No longer a grey, blurry ruin in an old photograph, but restored and far larger, grander than she'd realised.

It wasn't the front, but the side view of the house and what had been rubble in her picture was now a square tower, the stucco a soft, faded umber in the strong sunlight.

There were vines, heavy with fruit, trailing over a large pergola at the rear. A rustic table set beneath it where generations of a family could eat beneath its shade.

The garden was full of colour. And above the distant sound of a tractor, the humming of insects in the midday heat, she could hear water running.

The spring that had been their only water supply all through that harsh winter.

Her hands were shaking as she used her phone to take a photograph of the restored scene. Only the wall—Lucia's wall—had not been rebuilt. But why would it be? There was no one up here to keep out. On the contrary, it appeared to be a shortcut into the village and she glanced back down the path, wondering who the rather beautiful young man could have been. Family? A friend. Or an illicit lover, maybe, from the smear of lipstick on his lower lip, making his escape via the back way.

She took off her hat, fanned herself with it, turned again to look at the house. Wondering who lived there. Could it be the same family who'd owned the house when it had sheltered Lex?

Unlikely.

According to the website she'd found, the

Isola del Serrone vineyard had long ago become a co-operative run by the villagers.

And the glimpse of a swimming pool suggested that the house had been bought by some wealthy businessman who used it as a weekend retreat from Rome.

Whatever, there were no answers here. Only the wall was as it had been and on a sudden whim she turned, put her hat down and hitched herself up, spreading her arms wide to support herself as Lucia had done. Closing her eyes, imagining how she'd felt, the sun warm on her face, danger passed. A last moment of happiness before Lex was repatriated, sent back to his rejoicing family, and she was left alone.

'Well, don't you look comfortable?'

Sarah started, blinked. The man standing on the path had appeared from nowhere. His face was in shadow, his eyes masked by dark glasses so that she couldn't read his expression but, while his tone was neutral, it was not friendly.

'Am I trespassing?' she asked, doing her best to remain calm despite the frisson of nerves that riffled through her. He didn't look dangerous, but she was on her own. No one knew where she was.

'This is private land, *signora*.'

'But there's a footpath—'

'There is also a gate. Hint enough, I'd have thought.'

'Yes, but…'

'It was locked.'

'Someone held it open for me. A young man in a hurry.' Then, 'Hold on.' He was speaking in English. Sexily accented as only an Italian could do it, but English nonetheless. 'How did you know?'

'That you were here?'

'That I'm English.'

'Actually,' he said, mocking her, 'the young man, having made his escape, spared a moment of his precious time to warn me that I had an intruder.'

'*Warn* you?' She remembered him reaching for his mobile phone as he'd walked away, how she'd imagined him talking to some girl… 'What on earth did he think I was going to do?' she demanded. 'Shin up the drainpipe and pinch the family silver?'

Torn between annoyance and amusement, she had hoped he'd realise how ridiculous he was being. Maybe laugh. She couldn't see his eyes, but his generous mouth seemed made for laughter.

He did neither.

She'd left her bag at the foot of the wall and, without so much as a by-your-leave, he picked it up and began to go through it.

'Hey!' she protested as he took out her phone. The nerve of the man! 'Didn't your mother tell you that you must never, ever, under any circumstances look in a lady's handbag?'

'First we have to establish that you are a lady,' he replied, glancing up from his perusal of her messages, regarding her for a moment as if he was considering whether to search her, too.

'Don't even think about it,' she warned.

Maybe the silky scoop-necked designer T-shirt she'd teamed with cropped Maybridge market jeans convinced him that there wasn't room to hide as much as a teaspoon about her person. Or maybe he was saving that pleasure for later.

It was a thought that should have made her feel a lot more nervous than it did.

Whatever the reason, he returned his attention to her phone, going through her messages, then her emails. Pausing at one, he looked over the top of his glasses at her with a pair of ink-dark eyes.

'Have you found him yet, Sarah Gratton?'

For a moment she was mesmerized by the way he said her name. The vowels long and slow, like thick cream being poured from a jug. The man exuded sensuality. Every movement, every syllable seemed to stroke her...

'Him?' she repeated, before she began to purr. No... That wasn't right. She was looking for Lucia...

'The "dark-eyed Italian lover"?' he prompted.

Oh, great. He'd found Lex's email. But no one who taught a mixed class of teenagers could afford to betray the slightest sign of embarrassment. The first hint of a blush and you were toast.

You had to look them in the eye, stand your ground, come back with a swift riposte that would make the class laugh with you, not at you.

'Why?' she asked. 'Are you interested in the job?'

It would have been spot on if it had come out sharp and snappy as intended, but something had gone seriously wrong between her brain and her mouth. Between concept and delivery.

It was his eyes. Dark as night but with the crackle of lightning in their depths...

Under that gaze, sharp had lost its edge, snap had turned to a soft, gooey fudge and, apparently taking it as an invitation, he reached out, slid his fingers through her hair, cradling her head in the palm of his hand. There was a seemingly endless pause while she frantically tried to redial her brain. Send out a call for the cavalry.

Her brain was apparently engaged, busy dealing with a bombardment of signals. The sun hot on her arms, her throat, her breasts. The sensuous sweep of the mouth hovering above her own. The scent of warm skin, leather...

The world seemed to have slowed down and it took forever for his lips to reach hers. Somewhere, deep inside her brain the word *no* was teetering on the brink. All she had to do was move her lips, say it, but her butter-soft mouth seemed to belong to someone else.

When it parted, it was not to protest and as his mouth found hers a tingle of something like recognition raced like wildfire through her blood, blotting out reason. Her body, with nothing to guide it, softened, melted against him, murmured, 'Yes...'

It wasn't enough and she clutched at his shoulders, fingers digging into hard flesh as she began to fall back, leaving gravity to take them down into the soft thick grass on the shady side of the wall.

For a moment she could feel it, was breathing in the green, sweet scent of grass, herbs crushed beneath them. The weight of his body, the sweep of his hand beneath the silk, lighting up her skin as it moved over her ribs. Her nipple, achingly hard in anticipation of his touch.

There was a sickening jolt, like that moment when you were on the point of falling asleep and something dragged you back.

'Lucia...'

'What did you say?' he asked.

Sarah opened her eyes. She was still sitting on the wall, not clinging to this stranger but being supported by him, as if he thought that she was about to fall.

'Are you all right?' His voice seemed to be coming from under water.

'What? Yes…'

She was back from wherever she'd been, *whoever* she'd been—because she wasn't the kind of woman who invited total strangers to kiss her.

'This was where they said goodbye…' she whispered.

Lex had taken her photograph and kissed her and they'd made love there in the soft thick grass of early summer one last time before he'd taken the path down into the village. Flown away.

She turned and looked behind her to where her hat was lying in the grass. Not the sweet and green grass of early summer—

'Sarah!' the man said, rather more urgently.

'It's dry,' she said. And a little shiver ran through her. 'The grass.'

'It's autumn.'

'Autumn?' She shook her head, forced herself to concentrate.

'Are you all right?' he repeated, eyes narrowed.

'Yes.' Pull yourself together… 'Yes, of course I am.'

He touched a thumb to her cheek, his hand cradling her face as he wiped away a tear. 'Then why the tears?'

Tears? She swiped her palm across her cheek. 'Hay fever,' she said, grabbing for the first answer that came into her head.

'In autumn?'

Had he actually kissed her?

Her lips still tingled with a lingering taste of the perfect kiss but had it been a fleeting fantasy? A phantom conjured up by the place, by old memories, by her own loss?

She blinked, saw a tiny smear of lipstick on the corner of his mouth. Of course he'd kissed her. She'd practically begged him to. What on earth had possessed her?

There were no answers, but her brain finally picked up, answered her call for help. Speak. Move. Get out of here…

'I'm allergic to chrysanthemums,' she said, sliding down from the wall, forcing him to step back. 'It's hereditary.' Her knees buckled slightly as she hit the ground, her legs unexpectedly shaky beneath her and he caught her elbow to steady her. 'Great interview, by the way.' She took a breath, reached for her bag. She really needed to get out of here, but he was blocking her way. And he still had her phone.

'Leave your number with my secretary and I'll let you know.'

She'd made a stab for crispness but her voice could have done with longer in the salad drawer.

He continued to look at her for a moment, as if half expecting her to crumple at his feet.

She lifted a brow. The one guaranteed to bring a sassy fifth year into line.

Apparently reassured that she wasn't about to collapse, he said, 'Don't wait too long. I'm not short of offers.' But his voice, too, had lost its edge and the accent seemed more pronounced, as if he was having a chocolate fudge moment of his own.

'My phone.' She held out her hand, praying that it wouldn't shake. 'If you please.'

'When I'm done.' Then, ignoring her huff of outrage, he turned away, propped his elbows on the wall beside her and began to flip through her photographs.

They were mostly typical tourist shots. A few pictures of the school, her apartment. The kind of things she'd taken to send home or for her blog.

'You've come from Rome?' he asked.

She didn't bother to answer, instead leaned back against the wall to give her wobbly knees a break. Vowed to have more than an espresso and pastry for breakfast in future.

'You've been busy sightseeing.'

He glanced at her when she didn't bother to answer.

'I'm new in town. I'll soon run out of things to photograph.'

'Don't count on it.' Then, as he continued, found the photographs she'd taken of the wall, the house, 'What's your interest in my house? It's not an ancient monument.'

It was *his* house?

He didn't fit the image she had of a middle-aged businessman setting himself up in a week-end retreat. At all.

'It's a lovely house. A lovely view. Have I done something wrong?' As he glanced at her, the sleeve of his shirt brushed against her bare arm and the soft linen raised goosebumps on her flesh. 'I thought taking photographs from a public footpath was okay.'

'And I thought I'd made it clear that this isn't a public footpath. It's part of the Serrone estate.'

'You need a sign,' she advised him. '"Trespassers will be Prosecuted" is usual. Not that I'd have understood it. Maybe a "No Entry" symbol, the kind they use on roads would be better, or a picture of a slavering dog.' She should stop babbling right now. 'Give it to me. I'll delete them.'

'No need. I'll do it for you.' Beep, beep, beep. He still didn't return the phone. 'We don't get many visitors to Isola del Serrone. Especially not from England.'

'No? I can't say I'm surprised.' It was quite possible that she was the first English person to visit the village since her great-grandfather left. 'Maybe you'd do better if you were a little more welcoming.'

His eyes were now safely hidden behind those dark lenses, but the corner of his mouth tucked up in what might, at a stretch, have been a smile.

'How much more friendly do you want?'

And she discovered that, classroom hardened as she was, she could still, given sufficient provocation, blush.

'I'm good, thanks.'

He shrugged. 'It's your call.' Then, clearly unconvinced by her 'walk in the country' story, 'We're not on the tourist map.'

'That's okay. I'm not a tourist.'

'No?' He didn't sound entirely surprised. Which was surprising. Italy was, after all, chock-full of tourists and some of them must occasionally wander off the beaten track. Take photographs of views that hadn't made it into the guidebooks. 'So what are you really doing here?' he asked.

Until now he'd been in the shadows, a voice, a pair of dark eyes, a mouth so tender that his kiss could bring a tear to her eyes...

Now that she was back on the path, out of the sun's dazzle, she could see his face. It was hard to judge his age but his jet-black hair curled tightly in a thick mat against his scalp, his skin was golden, his cheekbones chiselled and his nose was so damn Roman that it should have been on a statue.

He was good to look at, but there was something about his manner, the arrogant way he'd kissed her, had gone through her emails, making quite unnecessary comments that—the blush notwithstanding—brought out what her mother would, in her teenage years, have described as 'a touch of the awkwards'.

It would have been easy enough to tell him exactly what she was doing but Lucia's secret was not hers to share. And, anyway, it was none of his business.

'You have me at a disadvantage,' she said.

That raised the shadow of a smile. 'Undoubtedly.'

She was right about his mouth. Definitely made for it…

'Having read my messages,' she said, making an effort to concentrate on reality, 'you know my name. I don't know yours.'

'No?' He responded with a slight bow. '*Mi spiace*, Signora Sarah Gratton. *Io sono* Matteo di Serrone.'

'Di Serrone?' About to say, *Like the racing*

driver?, she realised that would betray a deeper interest in the area than mere sightseeing and, back-pedalling madly, she said, 'You're a local boy, then.'

'I was born in the north of Italy, but my family are from this village.'

Turin was in the north. Was he the young son, orphaned when his father was killed on the racetrack? He had to be about the right age.

'You have my name. Perhaps you will be good enough to answer my question?' he said.

'Of course. Someone I know visited the village a while ago and he was so full of it, the hospitality of the people,' she added, heavily stressing 'hospitality', 'that I wanted to see it for myself.' It was as much as she was prepared to tell a perfect stranger. Almost a stranger. Not perfect... 'Has anyone ever told you that your English is amazing?'

'He must have been impressed,' he said. Then, the smile deepening to something that could very easily make a woman's heart beat faster, with or without the added kiss, 'Has anyone ever told you that you can change the subject faster than the English weather?'

'No, really,' she assured him, doing her best to focus on the view instead of the way her heart was in sync with the pulse beating in his neck. It was a little fast, suggesting that he was not as calm as he would have her believe. 'It's not only the idiomatic speech. You've got both irony and sarcasm nailed and that's tough.'

'I had an English nanny until I was six. She was strong on all three.'

'That would explain it. What happened when you were six?' she asked, but rather afraid she knew.

'She left, and I came home.'

'Oh.' Not what she'd expected.

He raised his eyebrows a fraction, inviting her to elaborate on that 'Oh', but, while his voice had been even, his lack of expression suggested that his nanny's departure had not been a happy one. No doubt it had left a painful gap in the life of a small boy. Better not to go there...

She shook her head. 'Nothing. She did a good job of teaching you English, that's all. Considering how young you were.'

'She was well rewarded for her dedication.'

Definitely something—and his 'I came home' was now suggesting, to her overactive imagination, that daddy had an affair with the nanny and mummy packed her bag. She really had to stop reading rubbish gossip magazines in the hairdressers.

'I took a post-graduate degree at Cambridge,' he offered, as if he, too, would rather change the subject. 'That was a useful refresher course.'

'I imagine it would be.' She'd bet there were any number of girls queueing up to give him English lessons. She sighed. 'I envy your ability to speak two languages so fluently. I'm doing my best to learn Italian, but without much success. I'm still struggling to order a sandwich.'

'Then allow me to save you the bother,' he said.

'Of ordering a sandwich?'

'I'd recommend something more substantial. You almost fainted, I think, and I'm not vain enough to believe it had anything to do with the fact that I kissed you.'

She'd almost done something, what or why she couldn't have said, but he was definitely underestimating himself.

'I skimped on breakfast,' she admitted.

'Always a mistake.'

'Absolutely.'

'And my rudeness could not have helped.' He looked down at the phone he was still holding. 'My cousin is an actress and we have problems with the press. Photographers.'

'I'm sorry. I had no idea.'

'No?' He shrugged. 'Well, Bella hasn't yet made the leap to Hollywood so your ignorance is forgivable. Perhaps you'll allow me to restore your faith in our hospitality by joining me for lunch.'

As he spoke, a woman appeared on the terrace below them and began to lay the table beneath the pergola. Without waiting for her answer, Matteo called down to her in Italian so rapid that she didn't manage to catch a single word.

The woman waved to show that she'd heard and he said, 'Graziella is expecting you. You cannot disappoint her.'

She could. She should.

Every atom of sense was telling her that if this was a movie she'd have been yelling at the stupid woman, dithering between going and staying, to beat it.

But she'd come to see the house and she'd never get another chance like this. It wasn't as if she'd be alone with him.

'I would hate to disappoint Graziella,' she said.

'And if you want to take another photograph,' he said, 'please go ahead.'

'Are you sure you don't mind?' A gesture assured her that he said nothing that he didn't mean. 'Well, to be honest, I was wishing that there was someone to take a photograph of me when you turned up.'

'Were you? To prove to your friend that you were here?'

He was frowning, as if he couldn't understand why she would want to take one in this particular spot.

'Yes. No…' She put her hands on the wall, using her heel against the rough stonework to boost herself up before he could help. 'Why wouldn't he believe me?'

'I don't know. But maybe, in future, you should be more careful what you wish for.'

'I don't know. This isn't going so badly.' She'd wished and Matteo di Serrone had turned up right on cue.

It hadn't started out well, but things were looking up.

Ignoring her somewhat provocative response, he said, 'Do you want to take off your dark glasses?'

'Oh, right.'

She pulled them off, propped herself on her hands, leaning forward, looking straight at her phone.

'Say…*formaggio*.'

She looked up at him, laughed, and he took the photograph.

CHAPTER THREE

ITALIAN FOR BEGINNERS

I went right off the tourist route and, as I stood in a village square taking these photographs, it felt as if nothing much has changed in a very long time.

Well, apart from the cars, satellite television, the internet and mobile phones...

AND so it begins, Matteo thought, as Sarah Gratton replaced her glasses. Hiding her eyes.

'I can manage,' she said, as he reached out to help her down.

'I don't think you should risk it in your enfeebled state.'

'I'm not in the least bit feeble...' He put his hands on her waist and her words died on a little gasp. Nicely done. 'You might want to hold on,' he encouraged.

She was lovely and trying so hard. It would be a shame not to make the most of the moment.

After the briefest pause she placed her palms on his shoulders. Her touch was light, her arms fully extended to keep a ladylike distance between them and yet the contact was like a lightning conductor, focusing everything primitive, ancient, instinctive into a single point of heat low in his belly.

And he was the one struggling for breath as he said, 'Ready?'

'Ready,' she said, poised, as cucumber-cool as if she were sitting on a bench in her own garden.

'Hang on,' he said, and she clutched at him, her fingers digging into his shoulders as he lifted her clear of the wall and she slid down his body until her feet touched the ground.

He held on to her, making sure she was steady. Then just held on as he was immersed in her scent. Not the kind sprayed out of a bottle, but something more personal. Warm skin, silky hair, the scent of a woman held in the arms of a man she desired.

For a moment it was not Sarah clinging to him for support. He was the one hanging on to her, weak with the longing to bury his face in her hair, her neck. In the creamy softness of the breasts he'd glimpsed as she'd leaned forward, bombarding his senses with everything female.

'I've got it, thanks,' she said, her hands sliding to his elbows, steadying him in return for just a moment before she stepped back to pick up her hat.

What colour were they? Her eyes. He should have noticed…

'Sorry. I'm heavier than I look,' she said.

She was a lot more of many things, but 'heavier than she looked' was nowhere near top of the list.

She glanced away, towards the house. 'I take it we're not going to use your brother's short-cut?' she said, laying her hand beside the tell-tale footprint on the wall. A good hand, with nails buffed to a shine. No rings. Nothing showy or obvious. Nothing of the femme fatale.

An innocent English rose taking a walk in the Italian countryside and if he hadn't been warned, hadn't been expecting something like this, he would have fallen for it.

'He's young, in a hurry,' he said, a little too sharply, and she turned to look up at him, a tiny frown plucking at the wide space between her eyes. 'There's a girl waiting for him in Rome.'

'Oh?' Her brows rose a notch. 'Well, he really is very beautiful.'

'We have different fathers,' he said, by way of explanation. 'My mother remarried after my father was killed.'

He wasn't telling her anything that anyone with a computer couldn't have discovered in thirty seconds. Always assuming she didn't already know his family history by rote.

'I see that I must add self-deprecation to the other gifts from your nanny.'

'Must you?' he countered lightly.

'It's such a very English trait.'

'Possibly.'

The only useful lesson his nanny had taught him was that everyone had their price. Never to trust a smiling face. Never to let anyone close. He'd forgotten it only once and he wasn't about to forget it again.

He took her arm—the path was uneven—as he turned up the hill. She didn't object, but then he hadn't expected her to.

'Age helps. And, being older than my beautiful brother, I've learned patience. The value of taking time to enjoy the journey.'

It was definitely time to slow things down.

He had lived like a monk for the past couple of years, concentrating on his vines, staying away from the kind of women who were drawn to celebrity. Who fed off it. Yearned for it. That had all been a game. A cat playing with a mouse. Until Katerina, he had thought he was the cat. He should have known better. Well, this time he was ready.

Almost ready. His head might understand that this was not real, but his body appeared to have other ideas.

'You're saying we should stop and smell the roses,' Sarah suggested.

'Why not? There's no rush. Is there?'

'I used to think not...' She shook her head, but she was smiling.

'What?' he asked, obligingly picking up the cue she'd dangled so temptingly.

'Nothing.' He waited, sure it was not 'nothing'. 'I was simply wondering if you're the kind of man who undoes the knots rather than grabbing the scissors. When you're given a present,' she added, in case he didn't understand.

He understood all too well and an impatient hormonal jig urged him to go for the scissors, but he reined it in.

This was definitely a moment for the careful unpicking of knots.

'I find that anticipation is often the greater part of the pleasure,' he assured her. 'Which is why we are taking the scenic route.'

'Oh? Should I be worried? About lunch.'

Inevitably the destination was going to disappoint her, but that was for him to know and her to find out. But lunch was merely the first stop on the journey.

'Graziella is an excellent cook. You can rest assured that expectations will be fully met, if not exceeded.'

The path wound up the hill for a hundred yards or so to a point where the countryside was spread out in all directions below them. The village, vineyards, his laboratory and nursery for the vines, scattered farms.

Sarah lifted her hand to shade her eyes as she looked into the far distance.

'Are there bears in the mountains?' she asked.

'Bears?' It was the last question he'd been expecting. 'There are a few brown bears, mostly in the national park. And wolves are on the increase. What makes you ask?'

'I thought Lex might have been teasing me.' She let her hand drop, looked down. 'The trees completely hide the house from up here.'

'It's tucked in a dip in the landscape. The winters can be hard.'

The only vulnerable spot was the broken wall. That, and a boy who happened to be in the right place, at the right time, to open the gate. Whether by accident or design he had yet to discover.

'Does the scenery live up to the recommendation?' he asked.

'Absolutely. Lex told me it was beautiful but actually it's breathtaking.' She looked around. 'Where's the river?'

'It's over there.' His chin was level with her shoulder as he bent to point out to her a glint of water on the far side of the village. Breathing again the scent of her sun-warmed skin. Something faintly spicy. Vanilla. Cinnamon. Good enough to eat. 'To the left of those trees,' he added as she searched for it.

'I have it,' she said. Then, as she spotted the motorcycles of the paparazzi who'd followed the limousine from Rome, 'Who are all those people down there on the road?'

Well, she could hardly ignore them.

'They're paparazzi. They followed Bella from Rome this morning.'

She turned to stare at him. 'Your cousin is here? No wonder you were so edgy.'

'It has been an interesting morning,' he admitted.

'And yet you were willing to let me take a photograph of your house?'

'I don't think the lens in your mobile phone would give you much of a photograph,' he said. 'But I'll let you into a secret. Bella wasn't in the car they followed.'

'So they're waiting down there while she's…?'

'Somewhere else.'

'Good for her,' she said, smart enough not to push it. 'Is it okay if I take a photograph?'

'Of the paparazzi? Or the view?'

'Sneak pictures of the photographers?' The idea seemed to amuse her. 'They'd just be a smudge in the distance. I simply wanted a shot of the view. Lex will be interested to see what it looks like now.'

'Will he?' he said, forcing himself to curb a snag of irritation that, while he was going out of his way to make life easy for her, charm her, she kept talking about some other man.

He waited while she took her pictures then asked the name of a town, its red roofs spread over the top of a distant hill.

'That is Arpino. Cicero was born there.'

'The man who wrote that a room without books is like a body without a soul.' She caught him looking at her and with a wry smile said, 'It's on a fridge magnet at home.'

'Then it must be true.' Forcing himself to look away, he said, 'It's an interesting place. They've recently excavated a well-preserved Roman pavement beneath the town square and there's a bell tower that has to be climbed by anyone who really wants to see a view.' Then, aware that he sounded rather like a guidebook, 'After a shaky start, I'm attempting to make a rare visitor feel welcome.'

'And doing an excellent job.' Then, with a sigh, 'Everything is so ancient here. We have old buildings, monuments at home, but in Italian history isn't a visitor attraction, it's embedded into the very fabric of life.'

'We've been here a long time,' he said. 'And while you were building in wood and straw, we were constructing in stone, which is more enduring.'

'You built in stone in Britain, too, but the Saxons were the original recyclers.'

It occurred to him that he should be grateful to whoever had sent her for having the wit to choose someone with intelligence as well as beauty.

The journey, wherever it took them, certainly wouldn't be boring.

'Shall we go?' He took her elbow. 'The path down through the olive grove is steep.'

'An olive grove? Hold on...' Now that she'd started, there was no stopping her and she made him wait while she took photographs of the olives. 'Sorry. I'm being a total tourist.'

She was certainly giving a great impression of one. But, then again, maybe she had never seen olives growing before.

'Don't apologise. Like life, we tend to take our surroundings for granted. It's refreshing to see the familiar through new eyes,' he said, opening the gate to the garden.

'Wow.' Sarah had stopped on the top terrace. 'Just...wow.'

Below them the vineyards swept away down the valley, but she wasn't looking at that. She was looking at the kitchen garden and in a moment had abandoned him to snap close-ups of zucchini flowers, artichokes, was stooping to rub her fingers against the herbs billowing over the path. They were swarming with Nonna's bees, but she seemed oblivious, as intoxicated by the scent as they were.

'You are a gardener?' he asked.

'No. That's my mother. She gardens, keeps hens and we've always had bees. What *is* this?' she asked.

He lifted her long, slender fingers to his face. He didn't need the scent to identify the plant but he was the advocate of taking time, in this case to smell not roses, but herbs.

'It is *Thymus citriodoros "Aureus"*. The golden variety of lemon thyme.'

'The Latin name. That's impressive,' she said, laughing.

'But I am a Roman,' he reminded her. 'Between Monday and Friday, anyway.'

Her hand was soft to the touch and his reluctance to release it was not entirely an act. It might be a game, but this wasn't the Garden of Eden and he wouldn't go to hell for picking the fruit.

'Of course it helps that I am a botanist.'

'Oh.'

'We don't do souvenirs of Isola del Serrone,' he said, bending to break off a piece of the herb, 'but put this in your bag and you'll remember us whenever you open it.'

Remember me, was the subtext. It had been a while, but he still remembered the moves.

She responded with every appearance of delight to this small gesture and he found himself wishing he could see her eyes so that he could be sure the smile reached them.

What colour were they?

Her hair was a warm chestnut, which suggested her eyes would be brown. But there were endless variations. Would they be shot through with green and topaz? Or dark and golden, the colour of the honey from Nonna's bees?

The sun was shining through the curved brim of her hat, throwing a lattice of shade across flawless skin, spattering sunlight across full, soft lips.

It would be silky to the touch, he thought. Her eyelids would be translucent, almost violet, her breasts, her thighs milk-white...

He took a step back before his imagination scrambled his brain, led the way around the house to the shaded terrace visible from the path. Calling out to Graziella to let her know they had arrived.

He turned to Sarah, who was regarding him with the tiniest of frowns. The look of someone attempting to listen to a foreign language, catch the gist of what was being said. And he wondered how much Italian she really understood.

'Lunch won't be long,' he said. 'What can I get you to drink?'

There were bottles of water and wine, both bedewed with moisture, waiting for them.

'Water, please,' she said, abandoning her hat and her phone. 'Is there somewhere I could wash my hands?'

'You'll find a cloakroom along the corridor on the left. It should have everything you need.'

He watched her walk away. Her hair, twisted into a loose knot at her neck, had worked loose and she retrieved a pin as she walked, tucking it back into place as if it was something she'd done a thousand times before.

The movement raised her T-shirt, exposing a thin band of pale skin. He was right. She was no sunbather.

The minute she was out of sight, he picked up her phone, found the photograph he'd taken of her sitting on the wall.

She was leaning towards him, her smiling mouth full of promise. The scooped neck of her T-shirt had fallen away to reveal a hint of breast. She really was very good, he thought, but then it would take someone very special to fool him a second time.

His temper had been stretched to the limit this morning. First by the uproar of Bella's arrival. Then the discovery that Stephano, armed with trophies for some girl who would no doubt be enthusiastic in her gratitude, had made his escape without waiting for Nonna to return from the village.

Matteo supposed he should be grateful that his brother had bothered to call and warn him that there was an intruder on the path that led past the house. Or had it been to ensure that he was in the right place at the right time?

His brother certainly hadn't mentioned that he'd held the gate for her.

He hoped it was simply because Sarah had smiled at Stephano. She had the kind of smile that would light up a cold day, if not a cold heart. The kind of smile that could make a boy—a man—forget, if only for a moment, what the gate was for.

She was not at all what Matteo had expected when he set off to intercept her. There was nothing obvious about her. Casually dressed, utterly natural, she'd been sitting on the old wall, face lifted to the sun, her full mouth smiling as if the day had been made just for her. Nothing to suggest that she was waiting for him.

The last time the trap had been baited, he'd taken the honey to the last drop, only discovering the betrayal when photographs of the private family celebrations of Bella and Nico's wedding had been splashed across the worst kind of gossip magazine.

He hadn't felt clean for months afterwards.

Now rumours that the marriage was in trouble, of affairs on both sides, were stirring up the same frenzy, the same tactics. Ironically, it was the woman who had betrayed him two years ago who'd sent a note warning him to be on his guard.

He'd ripped it up. But he'd taken heed.

This was a clever move, though.

Bella was a star in her own country, but nowhere else, and English language gossip magazines had no interest in her. Why would he be suspicious of an English woman out for a day in the country? Taking a look at a village 'someone' had told her about.

She had the figure, a mouth that promised heaven in a smile and delivered it in a kiss that would tempt even the most world-weary of men out to play. Add to that a rare touch of the innocent English rose guaranteed to arouse the dark side that lurked in every man and who could resist?

Her apology for trespassing had exactly the right touch of confusion and her indignation at the way he'd rifled through her handbag was utterly believable. Well, she probably hadn't expected that and the outrage was not an act. But the opportunity to flirt he'd fed her had been picked up with the confident assurance of a woman who knew exactly what she was doing.

He'd nearly lost it for a moment when he'd let his lips touch hers, drawn in by a rush of heat that had momentarily bypassed his brain.

Innocents did not kiss like that.

It had been a timely reminder that nothing quite so irresistible fell into a man's lap by chance.

Not that he planned on resistance.

If he sent Miss Sarah Gratton packing it would be only a matter of days before someone else would be on the case. He'd had it drummed into him from an early age by his mother, by Nonna, that with a big enough bribe, no one was immune from temptation. Including the nanny who'd been with him since birth. Who'd taught him to speak such good English.

No. He would take the bait Sarah Gratton was trailing so temptingly before him, play the foolish Italian lover to her cool English beauty. Let tiny snippets of gossip slip. Give her enough to keep her attention focused on him while his cousin and her husband sorted out their private lives.

And how long would that take? A week? A month? Longer?

Looking at the photograph on the phone again, the thought was not as unappealing as it might have been. In the meantime, he needed to know who he was dealing with and he sent the photograph to himself, to be followed up at his leisure, before replacing the phone where she'd left it.

He stood up as she returned, pulled out a chair for her, poured sparkling water into two glasses, handed one to her and raised his in a toast.

'*Salute.* To golden girls and glad-foot lads...'

'I don't...'

Grey. Her eyes were a clear silvery grey. Totally unexpected and yet perfect in a face that had been tinted a pale apricot by the warmth of the sun, rather than frazzled in its heat. Sarah, if that really was her name, very sensibly protected her peaches-and-cream skin from the sun.

'If my brother hadn't been hotfoot in pursuit of a girl,' he reminded her, 'we would not have met.'

'No.' She hesitated for a moment, then touched her glass to his, sipped the water. '*Salute.* What's his name? Your glad-foot brother.'

'Stephano. He's an art student. At least that's the theory. I doubt he actually does much work,' he said, demonstrating with his careless candour that all suspicions had been allayed.

There was a pause while Graziella brought antipasto for them to graze on and he opened a bottle of the golden sparkling wine that was the pride of the Serrone vineyard.

'You must taste this,' he said, pouring a little

into a second glass before she could refuse. 'The grape variety was bred by my grandfather. It was his life's work.' He swirled the wine around his own glass to release the aromas, encouraging her to do the same. 'There is a scent of herbs—' he took a mouthful, taking his time to allow the flavours to develop '—and a honeyed aftertaste, enriching the peach and melon flavours of the classic Frascati. It reflects everything that is Isola del Serrone.'

'You are clearly passionate about it.'

'A man must be passionate about something. My grandfather produced the flavour, my task is to improve yield and disease resistance for the next generation.' If only on a part-time basis. 'The Serrone vines have always been grown organically.'

She took a sip—how could she possibly refuse after that?—and her smile was unforced.

'It's delicious. Like drinking a summer's day.'

She couldn't have said anything more calculated to charm him. He would need to be very careful.

'I'd have to pay an advertising agency a fortune to come up with something that good.' He picked up the servers and piled cold meat, artichoke hearts, sun-dried tomatoes and olives onto her plate. 'How much will it cost me to quote you?'

'A piece of that bread?' Then, as he cut into the freshly baked ciabatta, 'I thought the vineyard was run by a co-operative. I looked up Isola del Serrone on the internet,' she explained as she picked up a fork. 'Maybe I misunderstood? I clicked on the translation device but the language was a bit mangled. Or perhaps there's more than one vineyard?'

'You didn't misunderstand.' He filled his own plate. 'My great-grandfather set up the co-operative after the war. He wanted to rebuild the community. Give the villagers a share in what it produced after all they had suffered. Give the young men a reason to stay on the land rather than join the stampede to the factories in the north.'

'Was he here? During the war,' she asked.

Again, not the kind of question he'd expected, but it was no secret.

'Francesco di Serrone was no friend of the Fascists. He was forced to flee to the mountains with the partisans when they came looking for him.'

'And his family?' she queried.

'His wife was heavily pregnant. The villagers hid her until she could join him, but she died of fever a few days after giving birth.'

'The world before penicillin. They were terrible times.' Then, 'Don't look at me like that.'

'How am I looking at you?' he asked.

'With that *what would you know about it?* look that men have when women talk about cars, or football, or war. I can change a spark plug, understand the offside rule and have a degree in Modern History.'

'I congratulate you.' He did not have to pretend to be amused. She was different enough to rouse his interest, hold his attention. Doubly dangerous… 'Perhaps you can explain it to me. The offside rule.'

'And do not patronise me.'

He made the slightest of bows. *'Mi spiace, signora.'*

His intention was to make her laugh, but she broke off a piece of bread, dipped it in the dish of oil.

'What happened to the baby?'

He told himself that it was the obvious question for a woman to ask. Something about the way she was concentrating a little too intently on the bread, however, warned him that there was more to it than that.

Was she testing him? Asking him about his family to see if he trusted her enough to talk openly about them. Or was she softening him up with questions he would answer without caution until it became a habit.

Or was he being totally paranoid?

It was entirely possible that she was exactly who she said she was and, having found herself coerced into having lunch with someone she didn't know—and he had not given her a choice in the matter—was simply grasping at conversational straws.

He would find out soon enough.

In the meantime, how his grandfather had survived his desperate start in life wasn't a secret. Nor would it interest a gossip magazine digging for dirt on Bella.

'He was cared for by a woman who worked for the family.' He broke off a piece of bread and realised that he was copying her own thoughtful dunking. 'She had a baby of her own, old enough to be weaned, so she fed him her milk, brought him up as her own to keep his identity a secret from the authorities until his father returned late in nineteen forty-four to reclaim him.'

'She nursed him?' It was clearly not the answer she'd been anticipating. Which begged the question—what had she expected him to say?

'Did you think they'd wrap him up in a blanket and send him to his father in the mountains to be reared on goats' milk?' He laughed.

'No, but you have to admit that it sounds like something out of a nineteenth-century novel.' She twisted a thin slice of prosciutto around her fork. 'Do you know who she was, the woman who nursed him? Her name?'

'She is not forgotten, Sarah. My grandfather raised a memorial to Lucia in the village church.'

'She's dead?'

What was that expression? Shock? Grief for a woman she'd never heard of until today? The story was certainly tragic but it had all happened more than sixty years ago.

'She was taken in a flu outbreak in the winter of nineteen forty-four,' he said. 'Along with her own little girl.'

'How desperately sad.'

For a moment he could have sworn that tears misted her eyes. 'A lot of people died, Sarah.'

'But not the baby boy?'

'No. Not the baby. Except, of course, he wasn't a baby by then.'

'No. No, of course not. Your grandfather owed her his life. Without her, neither of us would…'

She checked herself. And suddenly he was the one wanting answers.

'Neither of us would what, Sarah?'

CHAPTER FOUR

ITALIAN FOR BEGINNERS

The views are amazing. The mountains in the distance, which are covered with snow in the winter, are the Apennines, where there are still brown bears and wolves—il lupo, as we say in these parts—I'm working on my Italian.

The natives, however, are friendly. Despite the fact that I unwittingly trespassed on the local landowner's estate, he invited me to join him for lunch beneath a vine-draped pergola.

MATTEO was aware of holding his breath as he waited for Sarah to answer, aware in some untapped area of consciousness that whatever she said, it would be important.

Sarah, too, was utterly still, as if she was weighing up what to tell him.

'Neither of us would…what?' he repeated.

She gave the tiniest shake of her head, as if coming back from somewhere distant.

'Neither of us would be here. Having lunch together.' She lifted her hand in an odd little gesture that somehow managed to encompass their surroundings. 'The house would still be in ruins. Young men would have left the village. The vineyard would be owned by some soulless company producing wine to a formula.'

It was an answer. Deeper, truer than he'd anticipated. But she'd held something back and he felt oddly disappointed.

As if it mattered.

This wasn't real, he reminded himself. She wasn't real. Just some fantasy dreamed up by one or other of the many gossip magazines who had been making money out his family's misfortunes since he was a child.

'When you put it like that, a memorial plaque hardly seems enough,' he said flippantly. 'She deserves a statue in the square at the very least.'

Sarah frowned. 'Why? Isola del Serrone is a living, breathing memorial to the power of one woman's heart, wouldn't you say?'

'Would you?' he asked. Then felt oddly boorish in the face of her apparent sincerity. If it was an act, it was a very good one.

'On the other hand,' she continued, 'the fact that she doesn't need one isn't to say that she shouldn't have one. There are far fewer monuments to love than war and it wouldn't hurt to redress the balance a little.'

'That is true.'

'There's also the fact that women are desperately under-represented when it comes to statuary,' she teased.

'Consider it done.'

She snapped her fingers. 'Just like that?' she said, her intensity evaporating in the heat of a smile that lit up her face.

'Far from it.' And now he was smiling, too, at the idea that anything involving the village could be simple. 'The mayor will have to be consulted,' he said, 'and, if he is in favour, the deputy mayor will oppose it on principle.'

'Politics.' She rolled her eyes.

'Worse. Family. They are distant cousins.'

'Oh, dear.'

'There will have to be a town meeting, of course. Everyone will have an opinion and will demand the right to express it at length.'

Sarah was sitting with her elbows propped on the table, her chin on her hands, her fork held loosely between her fingers. A languid bee circled her, but she ignored it, utterly relaxed.

'Perhaps, if you came to the meeting and explained why you think it is so important, it would cut things down by an hour or two,' he suggested.

Or possibly extend it by as much, he thought.

Every man in the village would want to perform for her.

'With my pathetically slim grasp of Italian?' she objected. 'I don't think so.'

'It would be in a good cause.'

'True. And I suppose it would force me to make more of an effort. *Allora...*' she prompted, with an irresistible *how's that?* smile.

Dangerously charming...

'A good start,' he said. 'So, we are agreed. You will come and wring heartstrings?'

'How can I refuse?'

'It *was* your idea,' he reminded her. 'Of course it won't end there.'

'Oh?'

'The deputy mayor, having been voted down after endless debate, will ask the big question. How much will it all cost? And who is going to pay?'

'That's two questions. Maybe, if you invited your cousin to unveil the statue they wouldn't care.'

'Bella?' He was laughing now. 'Perfect. It will ensure photographs of them all in the classiest gossip magazines with the luscious Isabella di Serrone. With that as bait, they won't care how much it costs.'

'Well, there you are. All that's left is for someone to suggest a glass of wine and there'll be a stampede for the pub.'

'I'm beginning to think you've done this before,' he said, topping up her glass.

'I've sat on school fundraising committees. The first order of business is getting a local celebrity involved,' she explained.

'You have experience of committees?' He was beginning to enjoy himself. 'There will be plenty to choose from. The one to decide which artist is to be commissioned. The committee to approve the design and the materials to be used. And then there's the decision about the exact spot where the statue will stand.'

'And one to arrange a party to celebrate the unveiling. Hours of entertainment,' Sarah said.

He speared an artichoke heart. 'Dozens of lives touching and changing simply because we had lunch today.'

'Oh, I see. You're laughing at me.'

No.

'No,' he said. 'Truly.'

'We take our existence so casually, Matteo, but it hangs on the tiniest thread of chance. Often the weakest thread holds no matter what stresses are brought to bear. Others, seemingly strong, snap without warning,' she said.

'I'm not laughing,' he assured her. Well, maybe a little, which was rare enough. For a moment he'd completely forgotten why she was here.

Did he believe she was dangerously charming? When she had him laughing at the idea of inviting the media to the village.

Just dangerous.

Concentrate...

'You're right, Sarah. It is extraordinary. How many things, for instance, had to happen for us to meet?'

More to the point, what thread had snapped, sent her flying into his path?

He'd been leaning forward, was much too close and now he sat back in his chair. 'Why, for instance, did you come to Isola del Serrone today? Why were you walking through the village, up that particular path, at that precise moment?'

He couldn't have put his doubts more clearly, if he'd said, *Got you!* But there was no sign of guilt. No blush. No awkwardness. Instead she thought about it.

'It was the weekend,' she began, taking him seriously as she tried to fit the pieces together. 'I was all museumed out and I thought I'd visit the village.'

'Because your friend had told you about it?'

'Friend? Oh, Lex...' And suddenly she wasn't quite so relaxed. 'Yes. What about you?' she asked.

He allowed her to distract him. 'I was delayed. I should have been here first thing and if I had been on my own I would have driven straight to the vineyard rather than coming up to the house.'

'Because of the paparazzi?'

'And I had Stephano with me. We were in my cousin's limo.'

'Oh, right.' She looked suitably…confused. 'Actually, I was late, too. A friend looked up the train times for me and I meant to catch an earlier one, but I overslept.'

Another friend? Or the same one?

'And Stephano, who had no plans to be here today, slipped out the back way, opening the gate at the very moment you wanted to go through it,' he said, pushing the chain of coincidence as far as it would go.

'Why?' she asked.

'Why what?'

'Why did he slip out the back way?' she asked.

'Oh, I see. I suggested that since he was here, he might spend some time with Nonna. She had gone into the village on some errand and it seems that he wasn't in the mood to wait.'

'Maybe he was afraid that his golden girl would have got tired of waiting for him. Gone off with someone else,' she suggested.

'She'll be sorry if she did. He had a gift for her. A coat designed for Bella by Valentino.'

'That was the bundle under his arm?' She shook her head. 'One moment of impatience, a lifetime of regret.'

'You would have waited?'

She shrugged. 'Who knows what we'll do at any given moment? A step to the left instead of the right... One moment you're going along smooth as you like, can see your destination ahead. Then a tiny bump in the road throws you off course—' she looked across the table, smiled '—and, without warning, you're planning to erect a statue in the square of a village, in the province of Lazio, with a total stranger.'

'So not all bumps are bad,' he suggested.

A woman with an ulterior motive would surely have grabbed at the opportunity to flatter him, but she shook her head.

'Bumps are just bumps, Matteo. You wobble a bit, take the detour life throws at you and carry on.'

'Is that why you're in Italy?' he asked. 'Because you hit a bump in the road?'

'Not me. And it was a little more than a bump. The man I was going to marry ran into a rather sizable boulder called Louise. Now she's pregnant and I'm here.'

'Dislodged by the aftershock.'

He regarded her for a moment. She had her emotions firmly in control. There was no danger of her falling apart and weeping into her wine. But the smile no longer reached her eyes. It was as if a light had gone out and the day dimmed a little.

'She must have been a big woman,' he said.

'What?' It took a moment for her to catch on. 'No! I didn't mean that she was...'

'A "sizable boulder"?' he finished, when she couldn't bring herself to repeat the words.

'I was speaking metaphorically.'

'Of course you were.' He chewed a mouthful of something, taking his time. 'Interesting use of imagery, though.' He thought he detected the slightest crack in the self-imposed emotional lockdown. That classic British reserve. 'Round,' he said. 'Heavy.'

The corner of her mouth twitched, but only a glint in her eyes betrayed her desire to grin right back.

'Sizable,' he repeated, forking up some pickled vegetables. Not sure why it was so important to him to make her laugh. Only that it was. 'Boulder.'

He was rewarded with a snort, quickly contained.

'No, honestly. I only meant that Tom was—' Tom? Not Lex? '—knocked sideways.'

'Bouldered over.'

'Stop it!' she said, pulling her lips tight against her lips.

'"The lady doth protest too much, methinks." Abandon that English stiff upper lip, Sarah. She stole your man. You don't have to be *nice*.'

'*Nice?* Oh, that really is below the belt.' She

shook her head. 'Your English is much too good.'

'I once told an English girl that she looked nice. It was a painful lesson,' he admitted.

'Well-learned, obviously.'

'I return the favour to you. You are in Italy. We let our passions show. Enough with the metaphorical. Give in to your inner tigress. You want to scratch this Louise's eyes out. Admit it.'

She shook her head. 'No. It wasn't intentional. She didn't set out to steal him away from me. All it took was one look and I knew...'

'Nice Sarah Gratton. Sweet Sarah Gratton. Did you surrender without a fight? Give in? Did you actually care about this man?' he asked. Goading her, wanting to see what she really felt.

'Yes! Of course I cared—'

'How much? Did you throw yourself between them, fight tooth and nail? Or maybe you tucked them up in bed. Took them cocoa...'

'Stop it!' She looked confused rather than distressed. 'I cared, of course I did, but—'

'But nothing. Be angry. Curse his name. Insult her. You know you want to.' He leaned forward until he was within an inch of her ear. 'I promise I won't tell.'

He was rewarded with another tiny snort. 'It is true,' she whispered, 'that she could lose a few pounds.'

Not so much a growl as a mew.

Whatever she was, she wasn't a natural tigress. More a kitten. Or not as much in love as she thought.

Or maybe she was just a damned good actress.

She'd certainly got his attention. And, for the moment, he was more than happy to play along.

'Lose weight? Well, that's not going to happen,' he said, still a breath away from her ear. 'Not if she's pregnant.'

There was a moment of shocked silence and then her hand flew to her mouth as an explosion of laughter bubbled out, like fizz released from a shaken bottle.

You couldn't fake that and, as if to prove it there were tears in her eyes by the time she'd managed to control herself.

He handed her a napkin and she dabbed at them.

'You are outrageous,' she gasped when she could catch her breath.

'But I made you laugh. Which is far better than keeping your feelings under lock and key.' Talk about do as I say, not what I do...

'I suppose...'

'Far more satisfying than being *nice*.'

'Yes,' she said, with rather more conviction, and he wondered how long she'd had those feelings corked up inside her. Not that he cared, he told himself. Except that being hurt could tip you off the rails, skew your sense of self-worth, leave you vulnerable to suggestions that under normal circumstances you wouldn't consider. Easy prey for the unscrupulous.

Alone in a strange city, she could easily have met someone who'd spotted an opportunity. Taken advantage of her loneliness.

'So,' he continued, 'thrown off course on life's journey, you find yourself in Rome.' He nodded as Graziella appeared, indicating that they'd finished. 'Have you been here long?'

'Um…'

Sarah, still struggling with the reality of laughing at Louise, the fact that she was talking about what had happened to a man she had met no more than an hour ago, was relieved at the interruption.

She hadn't even told Pippa about Tom and Louise.

'*Grazie. Squisito,*' she said, risking her limited Italian as she smiled up at the woman clearing the table.

'*Prego, signora.*' There was a lot more, but she was lost after '*signora*'. That was the problem with practising sentences in the privacy of your own apartment. The replies never matched the ones in the phrasebook, or sounded like the ones on the CD.

'She was telling you what she's bringing

next,' Matteo translated when she'd gone. 'Pasta in a cream and mushroom sauce. Chicken baked with rosemary. A salad of some kind. Cheese. Fruit.'

Her groan was half pleasure, half torture. 'I'll never get used to eating so much at lunch-time.'

'I don't eat like this during the week when I'm in Rome—' Monday till Friday? She crushed a tiny flutter at the thought '—but it is the weekend. And in the country you have to relax, take time to live well. Eat, sleep when it's hot, take a walk through the vineyard when the sun has gone down.'

'It sounds blissful.' It was all too easy to imagine walking with Matteo as he checked the progress of the grapes. His hand ready to steady her if she stumbled as the dusk deepened. 'Unfortunately, I have a train to catch.'

'But you have seen so little of the area,' he protested. 'Enjoy your lunch. Rest this afternoon. I'll give you a tour of Isola del Serrone this evening. The vineyard, the river, the village. Everything that your friend has told you about. I will drive you back to Rome.' He paused. 'Or you could stay until tomorrow.'

The flutter became a tremor of something more like panic. They had been flirting, she may even have been indulging in a fantasy rerun of that kiss. But she'd been fooling herself. This was too fast. She was not ready. No way…

'That's very kind of you—'

He turned away as the pasta arrived, clearly assuming the matter was settled. Graziella tutted at the small amount she took.

'Mi spiace…' She turned to Matteo. 'Please, explain that if she wants me to eat everything it's going to have to be small portions.'

He translated and, as her ear strained to catch the words, she said, 'That doesn't sound anything like the Italian on my CDs.'

'It won't. Locally, we use an ancient dialect. It was spoken by the Volci who lived here long before the Romans.'

'And you still speak it?'

'I told you. We've been here a long time.' He picked up a peppermill. 'Pepper?'

'A little, thank you.'

'So,' he said, as they dug into the creamy pasta, 'you didn't tell me how long you have been in Rome.'

'A month, give or take a few days.'

'And you are enjoying it?'

'Great job. Great apartment. What's not to like?' she said simply.

'You have a job?' he asked, clearly astonished.

'Of course.'

'I'm sorry. I didn't mean to sound so surprised, but since you don't speak Italian...'

'I'm teaching at an English language school in Rome. Maternity cover.'

It was clearly not what he'd been expecting if the barely perceptible pause, an instinctive lift to his brows was anything to go by. But he was swift to recover.

'History,' he said. 'I recall that you have a degree in History.'

'It feels a bit like taking coals to Newcastle, to be honest,' she said. Then, because he clearly hadn't a clue what she was talking about, 'They used to mine vast quantities of the stuff in Newcastle. It's a saying.'

'Of course. I understand. But your degree is in Modern History.'

'I've become pretty familiar with the Tudors, since they're part of the curriculum. But not a Roman in sight,' she admitted.

'Are you enjoying it?'

'Yes, I am.' Which was true. The job. Rome.

'But you must miss your family. Friends.'

'They are a telephone call away. We exchange emails, photographs.' As if to make the point, she picked up her phone and dropped it in her bag. 'Chat on Skype.'

'It's not the same,' he pointed out. 'A computer can't give you a hug.'

She laughed. 'No, that's true.' And you had

to like a man who understood the need for a hug now and then. 'But I always wanted to travel.' She lifted her shoulders. 'I talked about doing a gap year, before university, but in the end I decided to be sensible, get the degree and the PGCE over and done with first, then travel.' Sensible Sarah. 'I had all the brochures, was deciding where I'd go, what I'd do, when the dream job came up. Too good to miss and when I met Tom on my first day it seemed like fate…'

'Everything set fair until he ran into the boulder.'

And she smiled again, not because she didn't still have the bruises, but what was the point in poking at them to see how much they hurt? It was over. It had been over from the moment Louise had walked into the staffroom. Forget the teeth and claws. Why would she fight for a man who had never looked at her the way he'd looked at Louise? As if he'd been felled.

Being mean was pointless. Louise had the kind of voluptuous figure that any man would swoon over. But Matteo had made her laugh about it. Who would have guessed that was ever going to happen?

'This seemed like a good moment to go back to the beginning,' she said. 'I signed up with an agency which recruits teachers for overseas jobs, got a reference so good from my Head-master that I suspect he couldn't wait to be rid of me.' She pulled a face. 'It's tricky when you all work together.'

'A decent man would have left.'

'He did, but he's head of sport. The kids love him. And I'm the one who always wanted to travel.'

'You left so that he could return to his job?' He grinned. 'I take it all back. You are not nice, Sarah Gratton.'

'Excuse me?' How much "nicer" could a woman get?

'Every day this man goes to work he will know he has you to thank for his job. And so will Louise. She won't be able to stand it. Sooner or later she'll insist he changes his job and he'll blame her. It's positively Machiavellian.'

'No!'

The chicken, golden-skinned and scented with rosemary, arrived at that moment, giving her a moment to gather herself.

It wasn't true. It couldn't be.

Could it?

Did that warm glow come from knowing she'd done the right thing? Or was that no more than self-righteous cant?

How many times had she imagined Tom walking down the corridors, seeing her everywhere the way she'd seen him? Missing her? Realising what a mistake he'd made?

Matteo dressed a green salad. Topped up her glass.

'No need to look so distraught, Sarah. You didn't twist his arm. The choice was his.'

'He loved his job.'

'So did you.'

'Yes, I did. But right now I'm picking up my life plan, taking the first step on my journey around the world,' she said.

'You are happy?'

Right now? At this minute? With the sun slanting through the heavily laden vines overhead. The soft murmur of insects, the scent of warm earth and Matteo di Serrone teasing her, making her laugh.

'Yes,' she said. 'I'm happy.'

He glanced across the table, holding her fixed in the power of his dark eyes as he said, 'Then let me say that I'm very glad you started your journey in Rome, Sarah.'

And she found herself saying, 'So am I.'

The chicken was amazing, a melting dollop of dolcelatte could not be denied, but she finally begged for mercy when he offered her a peach.

'Enough. No more.'

'You must have something. A pear? A plum?' Then, in apparent desperation, 'A grape?'

She laughed. She couldn't remember the last time she'd laughed as much.

'No,' she declared. 'Not even a grape.' But,

refusing to take no for an answer, Matteo reached up and plucked a huge dark grape from a bunch growing above his head. Held it close enough to her lips for her to smell the sweetness.

'Resistance is futile,' he said and she felt herself sliding into temptation.

Everything today had been about the senses.

Vivid colour, the scent of herbs and the sun-baked earth. The touch of a man's lips for the first time in months.

Languorous in the still heat of the early afternoon, lulled by the faint hum of drowsy insects, mesmerised by Matteo's dark eyes gleaming softly in the shade, urging her to this one last pleasure, she leaned forward the inch required to take the grape, closing her lips around it. Around the tips of his fingers.

The grape exploded on her tongue, the juice dribbling over her lips, over his fingers. And it seemed the most natural thing in the world to lick it up…

CHAPTER FIVE

ITALIAN FOR BEGINNERS

*I could make you drool, describing in
minute detail the home-baked focaccia
stuck with rosemary, the antipasto, pasta
al funghi, baked chicken, formaggio that I
had for lunch as the guest of a man whose
family has lived in this area for centuries. Who still speaks a dialect older than
Latin.*

*Tall, dark and seductively charming.
How easy it is to be seduced by laughter.
By hot, dark eyes and a smile that steals
your senses under the warm Italian sun...*

'SARAH...' She jerked, blinked.

Matteo's hand was on her arm and he was
looking at her with concern. 'I'm sorry. I was
afraid you were going to fall.'

'Fall?'

'You closed your eyes for a moment. The heat, a glass of wine...'

What? No! She'd only had half a glass. Maybe three-quarters, but her head was clear. She could still taste the sweetness of the grape juice, the warm dry saltiness of his skin as she licked it from his fingers...

Oh, right. Got it.

She might not have fallen asleep, but she'd behaved like an idiot and he was doing his best to save them both from embarrassment.

'I'm sorry. I should never drink at lunchtime,' she said, hoping that he'd put her flush down to the wine, the heat as she grabbed the convenient excuse. 'Half a glass of wine and I'm done for the afternoon.'

He shrugged. 'You're in the country. Eat. Relax...'

'There's relaxed and then there's falling asleep with your face in your food,' she said, doing her best to make a joke of it.

'There's a good reason why everything shuts down in the afternoon,' he said, pushing back his chair. 'Graziella will show you where you can rest.'

'No. Thank you.'

She was not sleepy. On the contrary, she was buzzing with adrenalin, her skin so sensitive that the slight movement of air as he stood up made her go all goose bumpy.

She'd lost track of time when he'd kissed her on the path. And now this. It was too weird and she had to go before she did something really stupid.

'Lunch was wonderful, Matteo, but I really do have to go.'

'Of course.' He didn't press her to stay and who could blame him? 'If that is your wish.' He eased her chair back, helped her to her feet. His touch on her elbow was electric and she practically catapulted out of the chair. 'I cannot, however, allow you to take the train by yourself.'

'Oh?' she said, dangerously. He'd given her lunch and now thought he owned her?

'If you will not wait for me to drive you back this evening—'

'I'll be fine,' she assured him.

'—then perhaps you would do me a small favour and allow Bella's driver to take you to Rome,' he continued, as if she hadn't interrupted.

'Bella? But I thought you said she wasn't here?'

He gave a little nod as if she'd confirmed something for him.

'She isn't. Stephano acted as a decoy. With sufficient bribery, my brother does a passable impersonation of his cousin. I came with him.' He shrugged. 'Largely, I have to admit, to ensure that he didn't simply drive straight to his student digs. I wanted them well away from Rome.'

'Stephano dressed up as his cousin?' She grinned despite her annoyance. 'You're kidding.'

'You did say that he is beautiful. In a scarf, dark glasses, with a coat thrown over his shoulders he can get away with it as long as he keeps his chin well down and his hands hidden.'

'The coat was a bribe?'

'A favourite from Valentino. He had to twist her arm very firmly before she would part with it.'

'I'll bet. And it explains the fact that he appeared to be wearing lipstick.'

'He had to make it from the street to the car with a mob of photographers only feet away. Don't worry,' he said, quickly, 'you won't have to face that. The car is under cover, invisible to even the longest range lenses. And it has tinted windows.'

'So why will they fall for it? Follow me?'

'Bella is a city girl and she loves publicity. She rarely hides from the press, which is why she gets away with it on the rare occasions she plays fast and loose with them. Her entourage will follow and you'll not only be doing me a favour, but the entire village will thank you.'

'Oh? Will I get a statue, too?'

'Maybe a plaque.' He watched as she shouldered her bag, picked up her hat. 'Are you sure you have to go? You've hardly seen anything.'

'I've seen enough.' She would have liked to have seen the plaque in the church, pay her respects. Walk where Lex had walked, but she'd discovered what had become of Lucia. It was enough. 'I have what I came for,' she said. 'A lot more. Thank you for a wonderful lunch, Matteo. And thank Graziella for me.'

'It is done.' Then, since there was nothing more to be said, he led the way across the garden to a garage block on the far side of the house.

The driver opened the door, but when she didn't immediately climb aboard, he moved away, sliding behind the wheel. Leaving them alone.

For a moment neither of them moved, as if unable to decide quite how to part. A handshake seemed too formal. A kiss, even on the cheek, too dangerous.

She opted for the handshake. 'Goodbye, Matteo.'

He took her hand, held it for a moment. *'Quando veniamo a contatto di ancora...'*

He released her hand, held the door for her. Whatever he'd said, he clearly did not expect an answer and she climbed aboard. There was a soft thunk as the door closed behind her and, before she had turned to pull down the seat belt, the car was gliding out of the garage.

She turned to look back as it sped along a road that skirted the vineyard and caught a glimpse of Matteo standing exactly where she'd left him.

What on earth was she doing?

He'd invited her to stay...

The road dipped. Man and house disappeared from sight and she sat back, fastened the seat belt as they approached high wrought-iron gates where scooters and motorbikes were already revving up.

There was a flurry of flashes as they swept through, but she scarcely noticed. She was too busy regretting her flight. Wishing that, for once, she'd had the courage to take the risk instead of grabbing the safe option.

She'd always played it safe. Done the sensible thing.

She'd talked herself out of the gap year, grabbing the safe job in her home town. Clung to the nest instead of spreading her wings. Fallen in love with the first man who'd made her heart beat faster.

If there had been a boy next door, she'd have probably settled for him.

Even now, working in Rome, she wasn't stepping out of her comfort zone.

Today, for the first time ever, she'd encountered something, someone, totally beyond her experience. Beyond her control.

She didn't know what had happened when Matteo kissed her, when he'd offered her a grape, only that her world had shimmered, slipped out of focus. That for a brief moment she had seen something, felt something that wasn't safe but exhilarating, intoxicating, terrifying.

That didn't just make her heart beat faster, but made it race.

This was not her world turned right side up, but tipped upside down and shaken.

For a moment she'd stepped off the broad highway with the way clear ahead onto a narrow path that turned and twisted through dark woods. Not safe, but the kind of dangerous, no end in sight journey that she'd always run a mile from.

She was running now, but even as she was driven in total comfort along the highway towards her well organised and very safe life in Rome, she longed to be back on the path through the woods.

Quando...

When.

Longed to be lying on soft grass in the arms of a lover, for the courage to give life everything she had, even if it was for a single day.

* * *

Matteo watched the car take the long turn out of the estate. Disappearing as the ground dipped, reappearing briefly, no more than a gleam of sun on metal.

'Your visitor has gone.'

He turned as Nonna appeared at his side. 'I didn't realise that you were home,' he said, kissing her on both cheeks.

'Graziella told me that you were having lunch with a young woman. I did not want to intrude,' she said, as he took her arm to walk her back to the house.

'It would not have been an intrusion. She would have enjoyed meeting you.'

'I have no doubt that she would have been polite enough to make me think so,' she said wryly. 'May I ask who she is?'

'Her name is Sarah Gratton. She's an Englishwoman who was visiting the village.'

'English?' She frowned. 'How did you meet her?'

'She strayed onto the estate, whether by accident or design I cannot be sure.'

She lifted her head, sighed. 'But you suspect the latter.'

'Bella is going through a bad patch with Nico at the moment. The sharks scent blood in the water.'

'I'm sorry, Matteo.' She raised a hand in a

helpless gesture. 'I hoped you had found someone.'

Hoped that he had managed to put the past behind him. Was ready to move on.

Rosa Leone had cared for him since his mother had left and he knew she was impatient to see him settled. Wanted to see a new generation of children running through the house, filling it with laughter.

'Bella and I are a sorry disappointment for you.'

'No. Never. I only want to see you both happy.' She caught his eye. 'The house seems very empty these days.' She paused, looked back across the vineyard to the distant road. 'She came into the church earlier. Your Englishwoman.'

'The church?' Sarah hadn't mentioned that, even when he'd told her about the memorial. Every time he began to think, hope, that she might be exactly what she said she was, something jarred the illusion. 'What did she want?'

'I don't know. Maybe to talk to the priest but there was a queue for the confessional. I'd taken some flowers to Lucia Mancini's memorial and she stood near the door, looking around. For a moment I thought...'

'What?'

'That I knew her.' She gave a little shiver, moved on. 'She didn't stay.'

'We were talking about Lucia,' Matteo said. 'I was telling her how she saved my grandfather's life. Kept him safe. Sarah thinks the village should erect a statue of her in the square.'

'For suckling your grandfather?'

'For saving the village.'

'What nonsense.'

'Maybe.' But it would give her an excuse to come back. 'Without my grandfather, things would be very different today.'

'That is true.' She laid a hand on his arm. 'I wouldn't have you, Matteo.'

Sarah had said something like that. Or begun to. *'Without her, neither of us would...'* She'd stopped, not because Graziella had returned at that moment, but because she realised she was going to say too much. What?

'Or Bella,' he said automatically.

'You are different,' she said, pausing at her favourite seat to settle herself in the shade. 'Is she coming back? The Englishwoman.'

Quando veniamo a contatto di ancora? When will we meet again?

'She said she'd got what she came for.'

'And what was that?'

He had no idea. He thought he knew, but a few photographs of the house, the view? The unexpected bonus of a face to face meeting with him? It didn't make sense. She should have stayed. Taken full advantage of the opportunity he'd given her to look around the house, the estate.

He'd invited her to stay overnight, for heaven's sake. He couldn't have made it easier for her.

Was she afraid that she'd gone a little over the top in her response to him? The kiss that had flared from nothing to a flashpoint of heat in an instant, leaving warmth that still lingered. Her tongue on his fingers as the grape juice exploded over her lips.

Or just afraid?

It was not long since she'd broken up with the man she had been going to marry. Some people responded to that kind of loss by flinging themselves into affair after affair. Others found it hard to move on as he knew only too well.

Had he got it so wrong?

That was the thing about trust. Once it was destroyed, everyone's motive was open to question. He'd even doubted Stephano, prepared to believe that, always short of money, he would let in the Trojan Horse.

But the worst of it wasn't his distrust of other people. It was that he no longer trusted his own instincts.

The desire that had flickered through him as he'd touched Sarah had triggered only a warning. He could not respond as a man should to a woman who aroused his senses. With his heart, with passion, with no thought of tomorrow.

Without that, it was simply sex. Meaningless. He tightened his hand into a fist as if to crush the memory of her lips against his fingers. Told himself that he was glad she had left.

He glanced at Nonna, but her eyes were closed and, leaving her to sleep in the shade, he went to his study, opened up his laptop and retrieved the photograph he'd sent from Sarah's phone.

He sat for a long time looking at it, trying to remember everything that had happened. Everything she'd said. Something was niggling at the back of his mind. Nothing about Bella, but she had said something that wasn't quite right...

Then, because he had to know the truth, he called up Google and typed her name into the search engine.

The drive back to Rome was swift and smooth in the air-conditioned comfort of the Mercedes.

Sarah told the driver where to drop her but as he came to a halt, she said, 'If I give you a note for Signor di Serrone, can you see that he gets it?'

'Of course, *signora*. I will leave it at the palazzo on my way home.'

He lived in a palazzo? Oh, wait. It didn't only mean a palace, but an apartment block. She lived in a palazzo herself and, really, it was nothing to write home about.

'Thank you.'

She scrabbled in her bag, found a pen and a postcard of the Spanish Steps that she had intended to send to her mother, and wrote.

Dear Matteo, Thank you again for today. I can't cook as well as Graziella but, if you're prepared to risk it, maybe I can return your hospitality one evening?

She added her telephone number and address and signed it simply 'Sarah'.

She read it through. It sounded like the kind of bread-and-butter thank-you note she would have written to an aunt for a birthday present. Not the kind of note you would write to a man who could make your heart beat faster with a touch. Who had shaken your world with a kiss.

Taking her courage in both hands, she scribbled a PS, then handed the card to the driver before she lost her nerve.

There was a flurry of flashes as he opened the door for her and she practically had to fight her way out before the photographers realised that she was not Bella.

There was a volley of questions fired at her.

Half a dozen men all shouting at once in Italian, but she didn't need the language to understand what they saying to get the drift.

They wanted to know where Bella was.

Who she was.

'Io non lo so,' she said very slowly in her phrase book Italian. *'Mi spiace.'* Then added an *I can't help you* shrug for good measure.

There were one or two angry comments that she was no doubt better off not understanding. A number of gestures that were unmistakable in any language. A wry smile or two that grudgingly admitted they'd been had.

She shouldered her bag and headed up the hill. One or two of the more insistent ones followed her, still firing off questions.

'Non parlo Italiano,' she said, over and over. Damn Matteo. She knew she should have caught the train.

One of them tried German, then French. She waved her arms, shook her head in a helpless *I don't understand* gesture but, even when they finally got it, backed off, she had the sense to keep going and walk right past her own front door.

How quickly you began to feel hunted, she thought, keeping her head down and heading up the hill.

At the top was the café where she stopped for an espresso and pastry most mornings on her way to work. By the time she reached it, she appeared to have shaken off even the most persistent of followers and she ducked inside, taking refuge until she could be sure the coast was clear.

'Ciao, Sarah. What can I get you?'

'Ciao, Angelo. *Un caffè freddo, per favore.*'

'Will you have a pastry?'

She shook her head, tapped her stomach. 'Antipasto.' She raised her hand a notch. *'Pasta al funghi.'* And again. *'Pollo. Dolcelatte... Basta!'*

He grinned. 'You haven't finished until you have eaten something sweet, Sarah.'

It was a daily battle between them. She practised her feeble Italian on Angelo, while he was determined to improve his already excellent English.

'I had a grape,' she said, giving up when she couldn't remember the word.

'One grape?'

'It was a very large grape.'

She could still taste it, taste Matteo's fingers on her lips. Would he ring? Probably not. And if he did would she have the courage to follow through? It was one thing to be kissed when you weren't expecting it. To joke about having an Italian lover. Quite another to actively encourage him. He might take her seriously.

She might take herself seriously.

'I've been on a jaunt to the country,' she said, to distract herself.

'Jaunt?' Angelo seized on a word he did not recognise.

'Trip. Excursion. Visit.'

'Jaunt,' he repeated, pushing his order pad towards her so that she could write it down. Repeating it while she dug out her phone to show him where she'd been.

The disturbance released the lemon scent of the sprig of thyme that Matteo had given her and she stopped, remembering the moment.

The sun, the bees, Matteo's sun-darkened hands as he'd broken off a piece of the plant for her. So much of today had been about his hands.

Cupping her head as he'd kissed her. Holding her around the waist as he'd lifted her from the wall. At her elbow, supporting her on the lane.

She touched her lips where they tingled with a memory that she couldn't quite pin down...

'Where did you go?' Angelo asked.

She snatched her fingers from her mouth. 'Here,' she said, flicking through the photos to find the one she'd taken of the view across to Arpino. 'Isola del Serrone.'

'Did you try the local wine?' he asked, sliding the iced coffee in her direction. 'It is like nectar.'

'I did. And you're right, it is.'

'And Isabella di Serrone.' He kissed his fingertips to the air. 'Her family still live there.'

Isabella?

'I had lunch with her cousin, Matteo di Serrone.'

His eyebrows rose and he blew on his fingers, then shook them. 'Whew! You mix in high society, Sarah.'

'No,' she protested, then let it go, unable to cope with explaining the difference between high society and celebrity. 'Is she beautiful?' she asked. 'Isabella.'

'Bellissima...' He put his hand to his heart. 'When she smiles you feel it in your heart. You feel—' he searched for some way to express his feelings '—you feel as if you have been kissed.'

Another customer claimed his attention and she looked through the photographs she'd taken, pausing at the one Matteo had taken of her.

She hardly recognised herself.

She'd wanted to replicate the photograph of Lucia and had done rather better than she could have hoped. Had she really looked at him like that?

Mouth, eyes with that soft, just kissed look. Leaning forward, almost offering herself to him.

No wonder he'd asked her to stay. He must have thought...

She blushed at what he must have thought. When he got her postcard he would have no doubt. And she groaned.

Matteo began his search on the website of the international school and there she was. Sarah Gratton, formerly Deputy Head of the History Department at Maybridge High School and now in Rome, covering for a teacher on maternity leave.

She gazed serenely back at him from a photograph that suggested absolute calm. A woman in complete control of her subject. Her world. It was a *trust me, your child is safe in my hands* portrait.

It was a very different image from the photograph he'd taken of her sitting on the wall above the house. Big eyes, a soft just-kissed mouth, that come-and-get-me smile. And, despite his certainty that she was the enemy, his response had been immediate.

He ran a search for Maybridge High School and she was there, too, listed on the school website as on a temporary posting to Rome.

She'd suggested they were eager to be rid of her so that they could keep her ex on the staff, but it didn't look that way to him. 'Rome' was a hot link and, when he clicked on it, he found himself reading her first impressions of the city in a blog she'd written. *Italian for Beginners.*

She was the real thing, he decided, smiling as he read it. And he'd bet this year's vintage that the photograph of her foot, with its slender ankle, in a pair of the strappiest sandals imaginable, had been for the benefit of her pregnant replacement. He had not the slightest doubt that the woman would be glued to this, hoping against hope that Sarah would find someone new and fast.

Definitely more than a load of old Romans.

Would her trip to Isola del Serrone feature in her next blog? Modern history as it had touched one small village in the foothills of the Appenines. Or an encounter with one of the resident wolves.

He bookmarked the page, then went back to the staff list. There was only one 'Tom', a brawny, fair-haired young man wearing a track-suit and an amiable smile.

He couldn't see them together.

No Lex, though. But that was surely a diminutive. Alex? Alexander? He couldn't find anyone on the staff list. Could he be family?

He checked Facebook, but she didn't have a page on that or any of the other social networking sites. Probably wise if you were a teacher.

He returned to her photograph. The wide, generous mouth, smiling eyes. She was smart, lovely, they sparked off one another like the national grid, and she hadn't taken any of the chances he'd given her to get closer to him, to his family. Well, maybe leaping at the chance to stay overnight would have been too obvious, but she hadn't accepted his offer to show her around the area, drive her back to Rome, either.

Having decided not to resist her, to keep her close, he was the one doing all the chasing. With the touch of her tongue still burning his fingers, she'd driven away without a backwards glance. She hadn't offered as much as a telephone number, an address, much less a hope that they might meet again.

Was she incredibly clever? Letting him glimpse a fathoms-deep reservoir of apparently untapped passion. Lighting the blue touchpaper and then standing well back while it fizzled.

Or was she exactly what she said she was? A woman still smarting from a broken relationship, not ready to deal with her own unexpected desire for someone new?

He could sympathise with that. He'd been there, done that, as they said. Had the scars to prove it.

Could he have got it so wrong? And, if he had, did it matter? If she was playing the long game, then he had to know. If she wasn't... Well, she professed to be looking for a dark-eyed Italian lover. He qualified on the first two counts and, as even a cursory glance at the gossip magazines would reveal, he didn't lack experience in the third. All he had to do was work out what would most charm her and, in the meantime, guard his heart well.

But there was no rush. He was just about convinced that she was an English school-teacher out for a day in the country, but he'd wait a while before he called and see whether she made the first move.

CHAPTER SIX

ITALIAN FOR BEGINNERS

> *...as the guest of a man whose family has lived in this area for centuries. Who still speaks a dialect older than Latin.*
>
> *Tall, dark and seductively charming. How easy it is to be seduced by laughter. By hot, dark eyes and a smile that steals your senses under the warm Italian sun...*

SARAH read through her blog so far, using it as a temporary distraction. Finding it nothing of the kind.

Should she say *a man*? Or would it better to say *a family*?

The last thing she wanted was for anyone to start speculating on who she had lunch with. What else they might have shared.

Or did she?

Matteo had implied that she'd chosen a Machiavellian strategy to punish Tom for his desertion. If she had, it had been unconscious and maybe, if he thought she had someone else in her life, she could put that right.

Or was that subconscious string-pulling, too?

Or was she just thinking too much? No one was going to be reading this. No one at Maybridge High gave two hoots what she was doing. Including Tom.

But that would be too cruel.

Instead, I'll tease you with these photographs of olives and artichokes growing in his garden, before I go out and indulge in another Italian passion. Ice cream.

'Sarah... How was your weekend? Did you get to—' Pippa winced as if thought was painful '—where was it?'

'Isola del Serrone. Yes, thanks. Your instructions were perfect.'

'Great. How was it?'

'Fine. Walked around a bit, took some photographs, trespassed on private land, as you do.'

'Oops! Were you chased by a hairy farmer with a shotgun?'

She laughed. 'He wasn't hairy and he didn't have a gun.' Deadly with a kiss, though. It was the kind you dreamed about. Woke wanting more... 'There was a slightly sticky moment until I'd convinced him that I wasn't a paparazzo sneaking around in the bushes. The fact that I was using nothing more dangerous than a mobile phone to take photographs seemed to do the trick.'

'A paparazzo? Good grief. Did you stumble across some celebrity's private love nest?'

'No.' The house, what she'd seen of it, had been comfortable, in the way that a well-used family home was comfortable, rather than luxurious. 'It's the landowner's cousin who's famous. Isabella di Serrone?'

'Really? Federico is crazy about her.' She shrugged as if she couldn't see the attraction.

Sarah laughed. 'It gets better. Once he realised that I was a mad Englishwoman out in the midday sun, he took pity on me and invited me to lunch.'

'A result!' She waited, then, when nothing was immediately forthcoming, 'Well, don't keep me in suspense. Good-looking? Married with seven children? Name?'

Matteo hadn't been wearing a ring. She hadn't looked but it was that hand thing again. Cutting bread. Dressing the salad. Big, capable, sun-darkened, with a touch delicate enough to pluck a bursting ripe grape. No ring.

'Hello? Earth to Sarah.'

Sarah shook her head. 'It was lunch, that's all. You?' she added quickly.

Pippa gave her a thoughtful look, but let it go.

'The usual. Clubbing Saturday night until stupid o'clock. Sunday cooking and cleaning. Looking at you, all golden glow, I definitely made the wrong choice. Next time you go exploring the countryside I'm coming with you.'

'The Roman pavement at Arpino has been recommended,' she said, straight-faced.

'Really?' Pippa pulled a face. 'You can have too much ancient history, don't you think?'

'I'll take that as a no, then.'

'What about the woman in the photograph you showed me?' she asked, as they reached the entrance. 'Any luck finding her?'

'Yes and no. From what Matteo told me, it appears that Lucia died in a flu epidemic in nineteen forty-four,' Sarah told her.

'Really? Sometimes life sucks...' Then, with a *got you* look, 'Matteo?'

Rats...

'She worked for his family. Wet-nursed his grandfather, apparently.'

'Eeeuw.' Then, 'So is that it? End of search?'

'Death is pretty final, Pippa.'

'But it's not the whole story, is it? Don't you want to know who she was? Didn't this guy tell you anything about her family?' her friend pressed.

'Only that his grandfather had put a memorial plaque in the church.'

'You saw it?' Pippa asked.

'No. There wasn't time,' she added lamely. It was too late to regret rushing away, turning down his invitation to the grand tour. She could have asked him to show her the plaque. It would have seemed perfectly natural after their ridiculous conversation about the statue. 'I should have lit a candle.'

'There's nothing to stop you from going back,' Pippa remarked.

'No…' Except that if he saw her he'd think that she was pursuing him. She blushed to think of the postcard she'd sent him. That he had ignored.

What on earth had come over her?

'We could go down there one evening,' Pippa suggested hopefully. 'With the Isabella connection, I am sure Federico could be persuaded to drive us.'

'I don't know. Lex didn't want me to do anything. Maybe I should leave well alone.'

'Of course. But let me know if you change your mind.'

Matteo stared up at the gap in the wall. While everything else had been restored, that had been left untouched. An escape route. He'd used it himself as a boy, a youth, sneaking down to the village to play, to meet girls. Innocent times. And maybe that was it.

Every man who came of age looked at it,

smiled to himself and left it for the next generation.

He turned away, walked up the hill towards the olive grove to see how far they were from harvest, his foot brushing the lemon thyme as he passed.

The scent brought him right back to Sarah Gratton.

She had not asked for his number, or offered her own. Hadn't called him, despite the ready-made excuse of the statue. Maybe he should have made less of a joke of it, but they had laughed a lot.

He stopped. Forget the excuses, he had expected a call, or at least a note to thank him for lunch. She was that kind of woman.

And if she wasn't, she could have called to ask if he'd found one of the tiny pearl earrings she'd been wearing. Or to wonder if she'd left her dark glasses in the car. Any one of a dozen excuses—he'd heard them all—would have done.

The last thing he'd expected had been nothing.

It was like waiting for the other shoe to drop and he couldn't relax. Couldn't get her out of his head.

He had begun to dream about her—her eyes, the silk of her hair, her skin. No amount of hard physical work as he threw himself into the week-long preparations for the harvest before he had to leave on a Europe-wide round of meetings could rid him of them.

'Plant life in tissue paper. It's someone's lucky day.' Sarah looked up as Pippa placed a basket containing a mass of yellow tissue paper on her desk. Handed her the heavy cream envelope that came with it. 'It seems that you have an admirer, Signora Gratton. Could it be that the not hairy farmer with a famous cousin who gave you lunch wants a replay?'

The first bell rang.

'Saved by the proverbial,' Pippa said. 'For now.'

Alone, Sarah opened the envelope.

A gift from my garden for your small terrace. To keep the pelargonium company. Matteo.

Heart beating much too fast, she opened the layers of tissue. The scent told her what the tissue hid long before the tiny dark-green-and-gold leaves emerged from its silky folds.

Not something expensively exotic from a florist but lemon-scented thyme, dug from his garden and placed in a simple terracotta pot.

Personal. Special.

It was only later, after she'd carried it home,

protecting it from the crush on the tram, had found a place where it would catch every last moment of available sun, that she wondered how he knew about the geranium. Pelargonium. Of course the botanist would use its proper name.

She'd mentioned her apartment, but she hadn't told him anything about it. About her terrace, or the plant her students had bought her.

He must have gone to the school website and from there it would be the work of moments to track her back to Maybridge High and the link to her blog.

She didn't know whether to be flattered by the effort, or annoyed that he'd checked up on her. Making sure she really was who she'd said she was. Or had taken so long about it. It had been over a week…

Oh, don't fool yourself, Sarah.

You're flattered.

He could easily have sent the plant without her ever knowing what he'd done. Instead, he'd shown her the effort he had taken.

She rubbed the tiny leaves to release the oils then, with the scent on her fingers, she used her phone to take a photograph. Okay, now her blog had a purpose. Where had she got to?

…Italian passion. With luck… Ice cream. Meanwhile, this plant—Thymus citriodoros 'Aureus'—arrived on my desk at

lunchtime, a wonderfully lemon-scented souvenir of my day in the country with a man who might have been prescribed by my great-grandfather to cure my broken heart. Tall, dark, with eyes that could make you forget your name and a kiss to melt your bones, steal your senses under a warm Italian sun. The kind of man to fall into bed with and think the day well spent.

Perfetto.

Well, that would give the Headmaster something to think about, she thought as, grinning, she uploaded photographs of the olives and artichokes in Matteo's garden. A photograph of the thyme he'd sent her, cooched up against the pelargonium. Just in case he looked again.

She'd just hit 'publish' when the phone rang.

'Pippa?'

'Are you sitting down?'

'Er…yes.'

'Well, hold on to your hat, sweetie, while I tell you something that you really ought to know about the not-hairy farmer who sent you plant life.'

'He's married?'

'Nothing so boring. The man is a Count.'

Matteo was at the end of a long day that had

been all about the commercial end of the business.

It wasn't his plant-breeding skills, or his new generation of vines that was his most vital asset to the co-operative. It was his title that helped to sell what they produced at the premium it deserved.

It had started in the vineyards with tours of the production facilities, the ancient caves where the wine was stored. There had been a suitably rustic lunch in the open, a picture opportunity for the buyer's website.

Finally, at the end of a very long day, he had wined and dined the buyers in the Rome palazzo.

As the last one was finally decanted into a taxi he turned to Bella, who had repaid his hospitality by performing like the star she was, making it an evening the buyers would never forget.

'Thanks for your help tonight,' he said.

'Just doing my bit. And I owed you for last week.'

'No. You can always hide out here, you know that. I apologise for being so bad-tempered about it.'

'You have many responsibilities, Matteo. Stephano and I are a great trial to you,' she said, looping her arm through his as they walked backed up to the first floor. 'Actually, the British buyer was charming. I'm taking him shopping tomorrow. For his wife,' she added when he gave her a sharp look.

'An experience he will never forget. Try to leave him with enough money to pay for the wine he's ordered.' He looked at her. 'How are you?' She shrugged, stepped away as he reached the door of his study. 'Are you and Nico on speaking terms yet?'

'I called him.'

'And?' he prompted, tugging at his tie, flipping on his laptop.

'And we have spoken.' She leaned against the door frame. 'So? Who is Sarah?'

'Sarah?' He repeated the name casually. As if the earth had not suddenly lurched.

He'd been trying very hard not to think about Sarah.

He'd been doing quite a fair job of it until he found himself describing his wine as liquid sunshine and was sideswiped by the image of her smile.

'Thank-you-again-for-today Sarah?' Bella prompted. Then, when he looked genuinely blank, she pushed herself away from the door, flipped through the pile of unopened post on his desk and pulled out a postcard, snatching it out of reach when he would have taken it. 'The "…I can't cook as well as Graziella but, if you're prepared to risk it, maybe I can return your hospitality one evening?" Sarah?'

'When did that arrive?' he demanded.

'I'm not sure. There's no stamp. It must have been delivered by hand.'

'She doesn't know this address.' Or did she? He'd told Bella's driver to take her wherever she wanted to go. Maybe she'd asked him to drop her off here. He could easily find out…

She put her head on one side. 'She knows Graziella so I'm assuming she's a country acquaintance.' She turned the card over. 'A tourist if her choice of postcard is anything to go by. One whose first language is English.'

'That's because she is English. She's teaching at the international school. I met her in Isola del Serrone last weekend. We had lunch together.'

'Well, fast work, dear cousin. You didn't leave here until nearly eleven. I have to admit I thought you were rather slow when that Swiss buyer made it plain that she was interested in more than your finest vintage. If I'd known she had competition…'

'It's not like that,' he protested.

'No?' She waved the card as if to fan her cheeks. 'So tell me, is she one of those cool English blondes?'

'No.' Not cool. 'Not blonde…'

'Brunette? Redhead?'

'Something between the two.' The colour of a ripe chestnut new from the shell.

'And her eyes?'

'Bella...'

'She has added a PS. Apparently, "you have made the shortlist".' She raised her eyebrows. 'What shortlist would that be?'

He resisted the urge to snatch the card from her hand. Betray an urgency that he'd been denying for more than a week. Instead, he smiled.

'She has a vacancy for a dark-eyed Italian lover. I thought, since I'm at a loose end, that I might apply.'

Bella looked momentarily startled, then she laughed. 'Okay, keep your secrets,' she said, 'but if this has been sitting here for over a week you should give her a call before she gives the job to someone else.'

'Bella...' She turned in the doorway. 'Have you decided what you're going to do?'

'Don't worry, I've got project meetings at the studio all this week and a ton of scripts to read back at the apartment. The field will be clear for you to woo your pretty teacher.'

'That's not—'

But she was gone and she was right. Her marriage was her affair. She and Nico had to sort it out between them. If the media would give them the privacy to work it through.

Not this side of hell...

The Serrone family had been their own personal soap opera since his father first sat behind the wheel of a Formula One racing car. The affairs, his turbulent marriage, his death.

The near destruction of his mother when the 'nanny diaries' had hit the headlines after the crash that killed him. Every row, every item of crockery that had been hurled, smashed, every argument relayed in lurid detail by the woman who was always there. His nanny. Printed in the gossip rags to feed the readers' prurient imagination. Making his mother out to be some kind of neurotic monster who wasn't fit to be the wife of a hero, the mother of a small son, until she broke down under the strain. The grief.

How much was that kind of betrayal worth?

And now there was Katerina's warning. Was it genuine, or was that just an attempt to get back under his skin? Did she really think he would ever trust her, or anyone, ever again?

He loosened his collar, sat down, read Sarah's message, written in a clear, elegant hand. He'd deliberately left it to her to get in touch, torn between wanting her to call and hoping that she would not.

So much for that.

This morning, before the buyers had descended on him, he'd got out his spade, dug up one of Nonna's precious herbs and sent it to her. A prompt, permission to get in touch,

or because he couldn't get her out of his head?
He couldn't have said. In the event, it had been
unnecessary.

Sarah had wasted no time in extending an
invitation to the dance. She must have thought
he'd ignored her note, wasn't interested. And
his response, when it had finally come, subtle
to the point of non-existence, must have seemed
like a gentle thanks but no thanks.

He checked the time. Too late to call her
now...

ITALIAN FOR BEGINNERS

*I told you about my weekend, didn't I? I
told you about the train, the views, the
garden I visited, lunch.*

Well, listen up. There's more.

A lot more.

*The truth is that I cheated you. Missed
out at lot of really interesting stuff. The
part about being mistaken for a paparazzo with my little phone camera for a
start. That was different.*

*And I cut the bit about being kissed by
a total stranger who is, let me tell you,
the hottest man I've ever met. Bar none.
And here's the really big news. Not only
is he the world's greatest kisser, but he's
a Conte. That's Italian for Count, just in
case you're wondering. The real deal.*

Not like one of those Johnny-come-lately blokes in the House of Lords. His family have been Contes for centuries. Lots and lots of centuries and you don't get many of those to the pound in Maybridge.

Not that I knew he was a Conte when he kissed me. I did mention that he'd kissed me, didn't I? Without so much as a by-your-leave.

Frankly, that's a bit off. Not the kissing—that was pure movie. You know, the bit where the man and woman just look at one another, the music swells to become throbbingly intense and cut to crashing waves... It's the not telling that I'm complaining about. I mean, how often is a girl going to be kissed by an aristocrat? I would have liked the chance to properly savour what is undoubtedly going to be a once in a lifetime moment.

He did earn a few Brownie points by sending me home in his film star cousin's limousine. I was actually mistaken for her for all of, oh, ten seconds. Shame I'm not interesting enough for anyone to pay for the photographs the paparazzi took of me or I'd be on the front cover of the latest gossip magazine and you'd be reading all about my love life in the hairdressers.

Actually, if they'd known about that

kiss they might start to get interested, because it seems that Conte Matteo di Serrone was quite a playboy in his time. Just like his father before him.

Contes, film stars... I am having a high old time here in Rome.

She would have to delete it. In a minute. Just in case there was someone out there, besides a neurotic Louise, who was actually reading her blog.

If only it was that easy to eradicate Matteo. Delete, expunge, obliterate the memory of a touch, a kiss, a summer afternoon. Eradicate it with one click of the mouse.

She was sitting on her terrace. Below her the great monuments of Rome were lit up and the traffic flowed around them in a hectic, never-ending sparkle of diamond and ruby lights but she was too angry to see any of it.

Savour the moment! If she'd savoured it any more they'd have been in the deep grass, ripping their clothes off.

Her phone bleeped, warning her that she had an incoming text. She reached for it, anticipating yet more silliness from Pippa.

Not Pippa...

'I've only this minute seen your card. Dinner tomorrow? Matteo.'

Bad timing.

A couple of hours ago she would have been all tingling excitement at receiving a text from him. Thrilled to know that the lemon thyme had been a spontaneous gesture and not simply a polite response to her card.

To think that she'd imagined he'd be interested enough to read her blog.

Clearly, the lack of any contact details on his card meant that the gift, charming as it was, had been more in the nature of a polite *not interested*.

But if he'd only just seen her card, then the one was not connected with the other. And his swift response implied that he was. Interested as hell.

All the delight in knowing that was tempered with the hot edge of anger that had been threatening to boil over ever since she'd discovered that, despite his formal introduction, he had omitted one very important detail.

That he was *Conte* Matteo di Serrone.

Anger that she'd had to keep tightly under wraps with a careless, 'I didn't know Italians did titles,' until she had managed to get Pippa off the phone.

Angelo, it seemed, hadn't confused the difference between celebrity and high society—and thank goodness she hadn't tried to put him straight on that one—but had known exactly who he was.

Her relief did nothing to lessen the 'idiot' tag lighting up over her head when Pippa passed on that little nugget of gossip, courtesy of her boyfriend.

It wasn't even as if he didn't use the title. She'd checked. Who wouldn't?

Google had obliged with images of the 'Conte' escorting actresses, models, glamorous females with matching titles to parties, galas, first nights.

Stunning in a dinner jacket.

Beyond belief desirable in white tie and tails with an order ribbon across his shoulder, hob-nobbing with the great and good at some diplomatic function.

With all that driving her, she didn't stop to think, but thumbed in her reply: 'Great. Shall I wear my tiara? Sarah.'

She regretted it the moment she'd hit Send. When had she morphed from Miss Sensible into...

'I don't know. Do you usually wear it in the kitchen? M' came right back at her.

...Miss Idiot?

Before she could think of a face-saving comeback, the phone rang. She put it down quickly, as if it might bite. Swallowed hard. She could ignore it. Leave her voicemail to pick it up.

Except that she was the one who'd regretted running from feelings she couldn't control. Who had written the note inviting him to call her. Added that suggestive little PS.

She grabbed the phone but, before she could speak, Matteo said, 'You are angry with me, Sarah?'

'No...'

'Do not be nice,' he warned her. 'Tell the truth. Teeth, claws...'

'Idiot,' she said, choking back laughter as her sense of the ridiculous at the very idea of her having a diva-ish strop overcame her annoyance. 'Of course I'm angry. You should have told me.'

'Should I? Does it matter?'

'The title? Or the fact that you didn't tell me?'

'Either. Both.'

'I don't care a tuppenny fig about your comic opera title, Matteo. But if I'd known about it I wouldn't have looked a complete fool in front of a friend who couldn't wait to call me and tell me that I'd had lunch with *Conte* Matteo di Serrone. I would never have mentioned I'd met you if I'd known,' she said.

'You wish to keep it a secret?'

'No. But, like you, I'd rather not be the subject of speculation.'

'*Come?*'

'Like your cousin, you appear to be something of a favourite with the gossip magazines, Matteo. And a bunch of photographers filled their boots with pictures of me climbing out of her car on Saturday afternoon. Not that I'm complaining,' she rushed on. 'Every woman deserves a paparazzi moment once in her life.'

'Do they?' He sounded doubtful. 'As for the rest, you have been reading old news. I have gone out of my way to avoid speculation for some time.'

She didn't answer. No one with a title and Isabella di Serrone as a cousin was ever going to be old news.

'I am sorry, Sarah. Truly. It never occurred to me that you did not know.'

'How? I arrived in Rome four weeks ago. I'd never been to Italy before, I do not speak Italian and, even if I did, it's doubtful that I'd have memorised the Italian equivalent of *Burke's Peerage*...' She stopped as her brain finally caught up with her mouth. 'You assumed I knew because you thought I was a snooping reporter!'

'I am sorry,' he repeated in English, then in Italian, over and over, his cobweb-soft voice like a caress against her skin until she finally begged him to stop.

'Don't. Please. I understand why you thought that.'

'No,' he said, 'you don't.'

She opened her mouth to protest, then realised that he was right. She didn't know. 'Do you want to tell me?'

'Another time. Right now, the only thing I want to do is kiss you.' There was a pause while she tried to remember how to breathe. 'Preferably without your tiara,' he added.

He'd made that sound positively indecent and a warm flush swept over her body. If this was what a dark-eyed Italian lover could do on the phone...

'How far away are you?' she asked.

Was that her? Flirting?

'Carissima...'

Matteo's voice caught on the word and she thought she might melt right there on her terrace.

She couldn't believe she'd said that. That she was talking to a man she scarcely knew like this. She should say something, laugh, but her breath seemed to be caught up in her throat.

The urgent blast of a car horn in the street below jarred her back to sense.

This wasn't real, she reminded herself. He was responding to her note, playing a game that she had begun. And that was fine. She wasn't interested in anything long-term. Permanent.

Been there, thrown out that T-shirt, too.

The last thing in the world she needed right now was to confuse hot sex with deep emotion.

Lex's prescription had been for an in-at-the-deep-end, no-commitment affair—something to raise her heartbeat, add a flutter of excitement to her life. Purely medicinal.

This certainly fitted the bill. Her heart rate was off the scale and everything else was fluttering fit to bust.

'I remember,' she said, doing her best to sound cool, calm, unfluttery. Miss Gratton of the Upper Fifth. 'Anticipation is the greater part of the pleasure.'

'Not, I think, in this case. Rather a case of delayed gratification...' For a moment the silence was as deep as an echo from space. 'It is late, *cara*, and don't you have a plea to my village's mayor to write?'

'I'm going to need help with that,' she said, and since they both knew that there was not going to be a statue of Lucia, or a plea made, that was definitely her flirting. Something she'd have sworn an oath she didn't know how to do. It was as if his kiss had jarred loose something in her brain... 'How long have I got?'

'There is no rush. We will begin tomorrow. If your invitation still stands?'

Last chance, Sarah Gratton...

'What time will you be here?' she asked, through a throat that seemed to be stuffed with gravel.

'Early, I think. There is a great deal to get through. I will pick you up at seven?'

Good job he didn't wait for an answer but murmured a soft, '*Buonanotte*, Sarah.' Something else in Italian. *Dolce*...? Sweet something. Sweet dreams?

She finally managed to squeeze out a husky, '*Buonanotte*, Matteo...' But she was talking to a dialling tone.

Lessons. She had to ask Pippa about finding someone to give her Italian lessons.

Matteo tossed the phone onto his desk and smiled.

His comic opera title?

Hardly the words of a woman intent on seduction. Very close, in fact, to what he'd been thinking himself before Bella had handed him her card. That it was good for nothing but impressing buyers of the wine produced in Isola del Serrone. And only then if the price was right.

Not true, of course. It went back generations, centuries, tied him to his family, the land. The vines that had been growing there when Rome was a scruffy little town of no importance.

And yet, intentional or not, she had prodded his dormant libido into hot, surging life. He had not been able to get her out of his head and tonight, when she had asked him how far away he was, his cherished detachment had been shown for what it was. A sham.

Carissima...

When had he last used the word to a woman in that way?

It had slipped out, no pretence. No play-acting at being the perfect lover. He had responded without thinking, flirted, teased...

It wasn't simply that she was a desirable woman. He met them every day of his life. Had spent the evening fending off a woman who once he would not have thought twice about taking to his bed.

Sarah wasn't just beautiful, she made him laugh. At himself. At her. Touched some part of him that he had buried deep. He not only desired her but he was, he discovered, in serious danger of liking her.

That was a complication he hadn't anticipated.

There was still the mystery of her interest in Lucia. The certainty that she was hiding something.

CHAPTER SEVEN

ITALIAN FOR BEGINNERS

> *When I was at school—dread words I know—I learned a poem about some old Roman called Horatius saving Rome pretty much singled-handedly from an invading army. I've forgotten most of it, but I remember declaiming this— 'And how can man die better/Than facing fearful odds,/For the ashes of his fathers,/And the temples of his gods?'*
>
> *I fell a little in love with Horatius and when I went for a run this morning, the mist, pink in the morning sun, lifted to reveal some temple built millennia ago that he would have seen in all its glory.*
>
> *Honestly, I went all goosebumpy.*

SARAH HAD SPENT A disturbed night. A tangle of nervous anticipation and sheets. What-the-heck-am-I-doing? clashing in a what-the-heck-

I'm-single muddle of half awake, half asleep dreams.

She didn't *feel* single.

She'd had boyfriends before she met Tom but he was her only serious relationship and deep down she still felt that she was Tom's girl. That kissing Matteo, wanting Matteo was somehow cheating on him.

Except when she was actually kissing Matteo.

When she was with him, talking to him she wasn't thinking about anyone else. It was as if her entire body was focused on him. What he looked like, how he sounded, how alive her skin felt when he touched her.

It scared her.

Light-hearted wasn't supposed to be this intense. Was it?

The minute the sky had begun to turn grey in the pre-dawn, she'd pulled on a tank and grey joggers that she hadn't even looked at since Tom had transferred his affections to Louise.

It had been a while. She was out of condition and the first mile hurt. A lot. Breathing was agony. Then, as the sun turned the sky pink, she found some kind of rhythm, hit her stride. Returning to her apartment slicked with sweat, glowing with satisfaction as she bounded up the stairs, she returned her startled neighbours' greetings with a cheery, *'Buongiorno!'* that no longer seemed foreign or strange.

After a quick shower, she deleted the blog she'd posted the night before, just in case anyone saw it, and replaced it with something that would achieve an instant switch off before going to work.

Pippa hunted her down at lunchtime. Looked at her through narrowed eyes, taking in a sleeveless, hip-skimming black linen dress she hadn't worn before, a peach ribbon-trimmed cashmere cardigan slung over her shoulders. 'You know something? You're beginning to look as if you belong here. You're getting that Roman look.'

'What's that?'

'As if you own the place.'

'It's amazing what an early morning run can do for you.'

Running was something that she'd done with Tom, to be with him, part of his life. Today, determined to burn off the midnight twitches, she'd done it for herself. And the only man on her mind had been Matteo.

'You went for a *run*?' Pippa gave a little shudder. 'And here was me thinking that it was all down to the attention of a good-looking man.'

'What good-looking man would that be?' she asked casually.

'I looked him up on the internet, you know. Good-looking barely begins to state the case.'

'Sorry to disappoint you, Pippa. We had lunch, that's all. I was home by six.' It would have been earlier if she hadn't been hiding out from the paparazzi but she wasn't telling Pippa that. She was already much too interested in her meeting with a Conte.

'Lunch followed up with a gift,' Pippa persisted.

'You saw it.' She'd insisted on seeing it, anticipating some floral tribute. 'A herb that I'd noticed in his garden and which he sent to the school because he didn't have my address. Or telephone number. He wasn't interested enough to ask for either,' she added.

It was the truth. As far as it went. He hadn't suggested they meet again. She had made all the running with that one.

'I saw the plant,' Pippa confirmed, 'and yet you have the look of a woman with the prospect of something more interesting than a night in with a good book ahead of her.'

'Have you never heard of the endorphin high produced by exercise? Come with me tomorrow. Try it for yourself.'

'No, thanks. I can come round this evening though. I talked to Federico, my boyfriend,' she added, as if Sarah hadn't heard the name a dozen times, 'and he offered to check a genealogical website for you. He could research Lucia's family without stirring up interest in her village.'

'I didn't think of that,' Sarah said thoughtfully.

'Well, it will all be in Italian. A bit beyond me, too. But if you give him all the details you have, he'll be happy to see what he can dig up.'

The bell rang for morning assembly.

'Terrific. I can't do it tonight. I've got a staff meeting and then a ton of marking,' she said, backing away in the direction of her classroom, her fingers crossed behind her back. 'Why don't you and Federico come round one evening next week? I'll cook supper.'

A staff meeting kept Sarah late, she'd had to pick up food on her way home and, as she opened the street door, her ground-floor neighbour called out to her, 'Signora Gratton!'

'*Buonasera*, Signora Priverno,' she replied as the woman took her by the wrist, talking twenty to the dozen as she led her inside her apartment.

This was not a good moment for a neighbourly get-together, especially one that was incomprehensible to both of them. She had to shower, wash her hair, do a hundred and one other things before Matteo arrived at seven.

Then she saw the box standing on the signora's hall table. The cream envelope with her name inscribed in a hand she recognised.

Signora Priverno was giving it the full action drama, the gist of it being that someone had brought this for her and she'd taken it in.

'*Molto grazie, signora.*'

'*Prego...*' She nodded happily. Then, 'Go, go...'

Sarah scooped up the box, practically ran up the stairs with it under one arm, dumping her shopping, school bag, everything on the kitchen table, hands trembling as she pulled off the envelope.

Had Matteo changed his mind? Sent a gift by way of apology? A great deal more than she deserved after her 'comic opera' crack about his title.

She pulled out the card.

The message was brief:

It occurs to me that you will have been working all day. We will eat out. Matteo.

She wasn't sure whether to be relieved that she didn't have to cook, or a bit miffed.

Yes, she had worked all day. She'd also planned a menu, raced around the market on her way home, choosing perfectly ripe pears to go with the tissue-thin prosciutto cut for her by Pietro. Bought steaks and salad leaves. Cheese.

A selection of miniature cakes. And now he'd high-handedly decided…

Stop it!

This was nerves giving her a reason to be angry with him. A reason to chicken out and tell him to get lost. Stay safely inside her 'nice girl' mould.

Matteo was being thoughtful.

She was being a prize chump.

The steaks would freeze, the rest would keep in the fridge. The cakes would go down well with morning coffee in the staffroom.

That settled, she opened the carton.

Inside, nestled in wood shavings, were two bottles of wine from the Serrone vineyard. No surprise. She'd already guessed that from the swishy shifting of weight as she'd hurried up the stairs.

That wasn't what had stopped her heart.

It was the bunch of huge black grapes that lay on top, cradled in a nest of the same yellow tissue paper that the plant had arrived in.

She ran the tip of a finger over the ripe curve of the fruit, plucked one from the bunch and put it in her mouth, crushed it with her tongue, letting the juice fill her mouth, reliving the warm-from-the-sun taste of it on Matteo's fingers.

Lost to desire in the heat, the sweetness, the desire for a man she'd only met an hour or two before.

Drowning in the sweet smell of the grass as he'd kissed her.

That sensation of being in another time, another place, where there were no restraints. Where only the senses mattered. If it happened a third time, in the privacy of her apartment... She swallowed. Matteo was right. Going out was definitely the safest option.

She put her shopping away. The wine in the fridge. Arranged the grapes on a small glass dish so that stalk where she'd plucked one didn't show. And felt like Eve standing in front of the tree, hoping that Adam wouldn't notice that she'd picked an apple.

Her phone rang. The heart-leap betrayed her, but it wasn't Matteo. It was the Headmaster of Maybridge High.

'Sarah Gratton.'

'Sarah. It's Giles Morgan. How are you settling in? Are you enjoying the job?'

'Fine. Thank you.'

'Good, good. I just thought I'd give you a call. I realise that perhaps I was thoughtless, expecting you to write a blog for us when you have so many more interesting things to do.'

Her mouth dried. She'd hoped that no one had seen the ridiculous blog she'd posted last night. Giles Morgan's emphasis on the word 'interesting' suggested that it was a hope unfulfilled.

'I just thought I'd let you know that I've removed the link from the school website.'

Oh, well, it wasn't all bad news.

'Whatever you say, Giles,' she said, using his first name, rather than his title. He wasn't her Headmaster, she would never be going back to Maybridge High and, instead of filling her with sadness, the realisation that she was totally free was liberating. 'If that's all?'

'Er...yes.'

'Then if you'll excuse me, I have a date.'

She ate another grape, then rushed off to shower, apply just enough make-up to make it look as if she'd made an effort, not enough to look as if she was trying too hard.

Did the same with her clothes. Lace against her skin where it wouldn't show. On top a simple silk shirt the colour of clotted cream, a pair of plain black trousers that relied only on cut and fabric to make a statement. A pair of glove-soft pumps.

Simple, go anywhere clothes.

She fastened her hair back at the nape of her neck with a antique tortoiseshell clasp that had belonged to her great-grandmother. Barely had time to check her reflection, panic that she'd played it down to the point of invisibility, when there was a rap at the door.

She took a deep breath, opened it.

Matteo was leaning against the far wall as if,

having knocked, he'd taken a step back. Put the maximum distance between them.

He said nothing, did nothing. All he did was look at her with those intensely dark eyes.

It was like being touched.

Her face, her lips. And too late she discovered that the silk shirt had been a mistake. It wasn't simple. It floated against her skin with the lightest of touches until every nerve-ending was shimmering with arousal.

Then, when she thought she might burst into flames if he didn't touch her, might burst into flames if he did, Matteo offered her a spray of pale yellow roses that he'd been holding at his side. And still he hadn't said a word.

'Thank you...' Her mouth went through the motions but it was as if all the air had been sucked out of her. She tried again. 'Come in. I'll...um...' She lifted the roses in a soundless indication of what her dry mouth was incapable of saying. She didn't wait, but stepped back, spun around, retreated swiftly to the safety of the kitchen, giving herself air to breathe.

She turned on the tap, considered sticking her head beneath it. Instead, she grabbed a jug, holding her fingers under the water while she filled it, taking deep breaths until she was nearly fainting from the rich, heady scent of the roses.

She cleared her throat, feathered the velvet

softness of the petals as she placed them, one by one, in the water.

'These are beautiful,' she called, when she finally trusted her voice. She sounded hoarse. She cleared her throat. 'And thank you for the wine.' She picked up the jug, took another breath, ordered her feet to take her into the living room. 'The grapes...'

Matteo had ignored her invitation to sit down, but had followed her and was now leaning against the door frame, watching her.

The jug wobbled and he took a step forward, rescued it, put it down, then looped his arm around her waist and pulled her hard against him. His gaze locked onto hers. Dark, storm-filled, thunder and lightning, daring her to defy him.

'I don't trust you,' he said. 'I don't trust myself.' And then he kissed her. There was no shimmer. Nothing dreamy or figment-of-the-imagination, shall we shan't we, teasing. No tenderness. Not a hope in hell of fooling herself that this wasn't happening.

His mouth plundered hers with a fierce, predatory hunger that should have been shocking, repellent. Instead, the heat of it surged through her veins like lava, burning away everything but her need for him.

Basic, physical, it had nothing to do with

white lace and promises. Happy ever after. Till death us do part.

It was raw, primal, but above all honest and she took his kiss, gave it back with everything she had, leaning into Matteo as if she would make herself a part of him. As if she could make him part of her.

It was the jug that brought the moment crashing to a halt as he turned urgently to fit their bodies closer together. It toppled as his hip caught the table, smashing on the tiles in a tide of cold water and roses.

For a moment he stared at the broken shards, the spreading pool of water, then, clamping his hand around her wrist, Matteo said, 'Out.'

'But…'

'Out. Now,' he said.

She looked back helplessly at the mess, but he headed for the door and she barely had time to scoop up her bag and cardigan before they were through it and heading down the stairs.

'Where are we going?' she gasped as they burst into the warm evening and, as if coming to his senses, he finally let her go. Pushed his hands deep into his pockets.

'Anywhere. Nowhere. Just out.' He glanced at her as they headed down the cobbled hill. 'Did I hurt you?'

'No.'

He stopped, looked at her.

'No,' she repeated, with a gesture that was pure Roman. 'I'm not being "nice", Matteo,' she said, walking on, leaving him to follow.

'I believe you,' he said, falling in beside her. 'Nice girls don't kiss like that.' He rubbed at his lower lip. Smiled a touch ruefully. 'You bit me.'

She'd *bitten* him?

He was right. She didn't kiss like that. At least she hadn't until now. But then she'd never felt like that. Been so completely out of control.

'Do you expect me to apologise?' she asked.

'I wasn't complaining.' He glanced at her. 'Do you want me to?'

'Complain?' she said, choosing to misunderstand.

'Apologise.'

Her turn to stop. 'No, Matteo.' She was free, unencumbered by any responsibilities except to herself. 'I don't want anything from you that you can't give me naked.'

'Let's go back…'

'I want a lover,' she said. 'A man who will make memories to keep me warm when I'm old. Memories that will shock my grandchildren. Make me smile when I'm dying.'

'We should definitely go back…'

She was trying to be cool, but he had this way of getting beneath her skin and she was fighting a losing battle against a smile. Who wouldn't want a man who couldn't trust himself alone in a room with her?

Any woman would smile.

'No, you're fine,' she said. 'You've already passed the physical—'

He practically choked. 'You are outrageous.'

'Am I?' He was right, she was. Tom would not have recognised her. She scarcely recognised herself. 'It's your bad influence. You are turning me into a diva.'

'I admit only to liberating the diva within. A role you appear to have taken to with genuine enthusiasm.'

She looked at him sideways from beneath her lashes. 'If I'm shocking you, you can withdraw at any time.'

'That, *amore mio*, is an offer you may live to regret,' he said, not bothering to hide his amusement as she blushed.

A woman, a *diva*, interviewing a potential lover did not blush.

Matteo reached for Sarah's hand, laced his fingers through hers and continued down the hill.

He'd followed through on her invitation to a no-commitment affair, something light-hearted, amusing.

Instead, he found himself perilously on the edge of something much more dangerous. That he couldn't control.

From the moment she'd opened the door, the cool, laid-back let's-play-lovers routine had been history.

When she had opened the door it was as if a draught of pure oxygen had been applied to his banked-down libido. Casual, light, amusing had burnt away in the heat of desire.

Only the smashing of the jug had brought him to his senses. Given him precious seconds to pull back from the brink.

And then, in the middle of giving a very fine performance as a sophisticated woman of the world, she, too, had lost her cool, blushed like a schoolgirl and he found himself...charmed.

'You do realise that an interview is a two-way dialogue?' he said, hauling himself back from the threshold of something he couldn't control. 'It's not simply for me to persuade you that I can deliver everything you need. You have to convince me that the position is worth having.'

She regarded him with a slightly baffled expression. The fact that he could see right through Miss Sarah Gratton when she was putting on an act was, if he'd needed reassurance regarding her probity, all he needed.

'Sex without commitment. What's not to like?' she asked, oh, so carelessly.

She had a point. He'd given a fair impression of a man with nothing more pressing on his mind but she had responded with equal impetuosity.

That they were not naked right now was down to clumsiness rather than design.

'If that's all you wanted,' he replied, responding in the same vein, 'you could go to one of the clubs in the Testaccio any night of the week and find a dozen young men happy to oblige.'

'If I'd wanted a one-night stand I wouldn't have had to come to Rome,' she snapped, and he laughed as the real Sarah Gratton showed up.

'*Brava, carissima.* I stand corrected.'

She stopped, took a breath. 'No. You're right. Hands up, you've got me. I've never done anything like this before,' she said, the bold diva morphing into someone much less certain of herself.

'That, *cara*, is obvious.'

While he had done it too many times. The flowers, the little notes, all the tender little touches that made a woman melt.

'So? What do I have to do?' she asked. 'To persuade you.'

'To have an affair with you?'

Was she serious?

Was he?

What on earth was he doing here? Cynical, suspicious, unfeeling, she could not have chosen a worse man for the kind of light-hearted affair with which to heal her broken heart.

Or maybe not.

He had once known exactly how to make a woman feel adored. She'd seen the evidence for herself when she'd searched the Net, looking for him. As he'd looked for her. The playboy Conte, following in the family tradition of making the gossip magazine editors' day. 'Why don't you start by telling me three things about yourself that I don't know?' he began.

She frowned. 'What sort of things?'

'It doesn't matter.'

'Oh, I see. Psychological games.'

'Isn't that what makes a relationship interesting? The games we play with each other?' He felt a tiny shiver run through her. 'Don't think too hard,' he warned.

'My middle name is Florence,' she offered. Playing safe.

'You were named after Florence Nightingale?'

'No, after my grandmother. Although, since she was the first person to be called that, I suppose technically we are all named after her.'

'Florence Nightingale?'

'Yes. She was born in Florence. People thought it very odd of her parents to name her after the city, but they'd already done it with her sister.' She paused. 'She was born in Naples.'

'It's fortunate that she didn't become the legend, then, or your middle name would be Parthenope.'

She dug her elbow in his ribs. 'That was *my* line.'

He grinned, took her arm and tucked it beneath his so that they were closer. 'Next?'

'I'm allergic to spinach. It contains some chemical that makes me sick.'

About to tell her what it was, he thought better of it.

'You must be inconsolable,' he said, easing her towards a pavement café.

'Very nearly,' she said seriously, but her eyes were laughing.

How could he have ever doubted her sincerity?

It was early and a hovering waiter whipped out a chair for her. He ordered wine, mineral water and the man left the menus and melted away.

'What is your third unknown?'

'I'm left-handed.'

He shook his head. 'I already knew that.'

'Did you?' She was clearly surprised that he should have noticed.

'You were holding your phone in your left hand when I first saw you,' he said. 'Sitting on the wall, your face lifted to the sun.'

She curled her fingers into her palm self-consciously and he took her hand, smoothed it flat across his palm with a sweep of his thumb across her fingers.

'It might have been chance,' she said.

'You took the roses I brought you with your left hand,' he said.

'Poor things. I should have picked them up, put them in water.'

'If we had stayed in your apartment you wouldn't have been thinking about roses.'

Her lids swept down over her eyes, a touch of colour returned to her cheeks. 'No,' she admitted.

'And it was your left hand that you raised when I kissed you,' he said. 'The fingers of your left hand that curled around my neck, that slid through my hair.'

Her left hand that had held him as she'd leaned into him, pressing her breasts against his chest, fitting her hips into his.

Cradled in his, her hand trembled. Or was it his?

'You have excellent observational skills,' she said with remarkable control, but nowhere near as bold as she would have him think.

Maybe.

Or maybe he'd been looking too hard. Seeing everything and seeing nothing. Looking for complication when there was only simplicity.

For lies when there was only truth. As once he'd seen truth when there were only lies.

'Try again,' he invited, wanting to know everything about Sarah Gratton.

She looked at him for a long moment, then shook her head. 'Why don't you trust me, Matteo?'

He didn't reply.

'I'm a teacher,' she went on, when he didn't immediately answer. 'You know that. You've used the internet to check for yourself that I haven't made it all up. And yet you still said, "I don't trust you…"'

'I also said that I didn't trust myself,' he reminded her. 'Before I kissed you.'

Remind her of that. The intensity of it. The passion. They would have been in bed now— always assuming they would have made it that far—if he hadn't hauled her out of the flat.

She shook her head. 'That is different.'

His silence conceded the point.

'You said you would tell me why,' she pressed when he didn't answer.

'I did,' he admitted. 'I had intended that we would sit on your little terrace this evening, drink a glass of wine, eat an olive or two like civilised people and I would tell you the whole sordid sorry story.'

Then she'd opened the door, slightly flushed, breathless, the gossamer-fine silk of her shirt moulding itself to her body in the movement of air, and his careful plans had gone right out of his head.

'I'll tell you now.'

'No. Wait.' She looked down at the table. At their intertwined hands. 'First I have to tell you the most important thing you don't know about me, Matteo.' She lifted her head, looked straight at him, her clear grey eyes swirling with mist. 'I lied about why I came to Isola del Serrone.'

CHAPTER EIGHT

ITALIAN FOR BEGINNERS

*Eating out in Italy is an event with entire
families, from grandparents to the young-
est babies, gathered around a restaurant
table. They talk, they gesture, they laugh,
sharing precious time together.*

*Young people meet their friends, have
an espresso or a glass of wine, or even a
bowl of chips at a small street café. It is
one of the great civilising pleasures of a
climate where rain is the exception rather
than the rule...*

MATTEO'S thumb, which had been rubbing
gently at the back of her fingers, stopped
moving. Everything stopped moving. The traffic. The noise and movement around them in
the café. His heart.

'Lied?'

Yes. No...

Everything he knew about her screamed a denial. And yet, despite all the truths he had uncovered, he had always known that there was more to Sarah's visit to Isola del Serrone than a day trip on the recommendation of a friend.

'So?' he asked, his voice steadier than the pulse thrumming through his head. 'Why did you come?'

'Lex did tell me about the village,' she began, 'and I wanted to see it. Wanted to be able to tell him what it looks like now. That it is a good place.' Her words came out in a rush. 'But I came to find the house, too. Your house.'

His hand tightened around hers, as if to hang on to the promise of something sweet that was slipping away...

But she was looking at him across the table, her eyes so grave, so beautiful. Her mouth full, swollen from the passion of the kiss they had shared and right at this moment he was wishing that he had stayed in her apartment. Followed that kiss through to its inevitable conclusion. That he was in bed with her, where words had no meaning beyond the moment they were uttered.

'It's why I climbed the hill,' she said. 'I thought if I was high up, I could look down on the village and I would see it.'

'You were right,' he said, hearing the calm detachment with which he spoke. So at odds

with the painful thumping of his heart. Unfeeling? Did he think that he was unfeeling?
He had been feeling from the moment he'd
surprised Sarah, kissed her. Had been thinking about her for more than a week. Then last
night... It was hardly surprising that he'd gone
off like a firecracker the minute he'd set eyes
on her.

'I expected to see a ruin...'

A ruin? And, like a slipping cog finally en-
gaging with a wheel, the niggle at the back of
his brain that had been bothering him since that
Saturday finally slotted into place.

'...but then I found the wall and there it was.
Rebuilt. Surrounded by flowers. Beautiful.'

When Sarah had been talking about chance,
consequences, she had said that if his grandfather hadn't survived, the house would 'still be a
ruins'. For that she had to know that it had once
been one. Long ago. Before either of them was
born.

'Who is Lex?' he demanded, no longer de-
tached or calm.

She blinked at his fierceness. 'My great-
grandfather.'

'Great?'

The waiter arrived with the wine and he
waved impatiently at him to leave it, not bothering to check the label, the temperature.

It was left to Sarah to smile her thanks.

'He's your *great*-grandfather?' he repeated. 'How long ago was he there? In the village? At the villa?'

'It's been a while,' she said. 'He's ninety next birthday, although he's still active. He plays chess online. Takes the occasional cruise. He likes to tease my mother. He tells her that he's looking for a merry widow—'

'How long is a while?' he demanded, cutting her short.

He saw her take a steadying breath and knew the answer a split second before she told him.

'It was nineteen forty-four.'

'He was a soldier?' One of the liberating army who had been welcomed with dancing in the streets.

'No. A pilot. Flying reconnaissance missions. Taking photographs from the air. His engine failed and he had to bail out. A young woman found him, frozen, starving. She took care of him, kept him safe for months until the Allies arrived.'

Months?

'I have never heard this story.'

'I grew up with it. She hid him in what was left of your house.'

'That must have been grim,' he said.

'Better than the alternative. And I don't suppose everyone would have been happy to know they were sheltering an enemy in their midst.'

'By then we were fighting the same enemy.'

'Even so. If you had a husband or son who had been wounded or killed, who was a prisoner…'

He thought about it, as she clearly had.

'You're right. The fewer people who knew he was there the better. But this woman was risking everything. She must have had a heart as big as a house.'

'And she had that ageless beauty. Lex had a photograph of her sitting on the wall exactly where you found me.'

'You said her name. When I kissed you. Lucia…' Now it made sense. Sarah's passion, the shadow that had crossed her face when she learned that Lucia was dead.

'She felt so close.' She shook her head. 'I can't describe it but for a moment it was as if I was her. Saying goodbye to him. Knowing that she would never see him again.'

'You were thinking about her,' he said, attempting to rationalise it. 'Thinking about them both.'

'Yes.' She shook her head. 'Lex didn't want me to come. He said it was a mistake to stir up old memories. Maybe he's right.'

'No. We must remember, always.'

'He remembers. He kept the photograph she gave him hidden away. He only showed me when I said I was coming to Rome.'

'They were lovers,' he stated.

'Oh, yes.'

'*Amore vietato*. Forbidden love is often the sweetest. Will you tell him what you have found?'

She shook her head. 'No. It would make him unhappy to know that she'd died so soon after he'd left her. He sent money after he'd got back, but he would feel guilty that he hadn't done more. He was studying to be a doctor when the war started.'

'Did he finish his studies?'

'Yes. He had his life. A wife, a family. All the things she was denied.'

'You're right not to tell him,' Matteo said, aware that a massive weight had been lifted from him. His instincts about Sarah had been right.

Sarah was an English schoolteacher who had been digging into the past to find a story that involved her own family. That it had touched his, over sixty years ago, was pure chance. She had blundered into his life in one of those happy accidents that occurred when everything came together in one place.

As Lucia had found Lex, he had found Sarah and his fingers folded around hers.

'What is indisputable is that without her, *amore mio*, neither of us would be here,' he said, lifting her fingers to his lips. 'When you come to Isola del Serrone again, we will light a candle. *Per amore. Per luce.* For love. For light.'

Sarah could not have said what she ate, only that they sat for a long time, talking about nothing and everything. Her childhood. Her older brothers who, unlike her, had flown the nest at the first possible moment, working abroad. Settling in Canada and New Zealand. About her mother's garden. Visiting the bees to tell them she was leaving.

'You talk to your bees?' he asked, smiling.

'Of course. They are family. You have to tell them everything or they'll desert you.'

'Will they?'

'Maybe it's just stroppy English bees.'

'No, I don't think so. Nonna always visits the hives when she has something on her mind. Sits with them,' he admitted.

'Lex does that, too. He says that they listen.'

'It's a family thing? Bee-keeping.'

'Oh, yes. Lex started keeping them after the war. Because of the shortages, rationing, I suppose.'

'Do you want anything else, or shall we walk for a while?' he asked.

He settled the bill and his hand in hers, they headed into the street.

'Tell me about you, Matteo. Same deal. Three things that I don't know about you.'

'My father was a Formula One racing driver,' he said. 'Or maybe you already know that from your friend's web searches?'

'I do, but not from Pippa. Francesco di Serrone's name came up when I was looking for the village. He was named after his grandfather? The man who took to the mountains?'

'*Certo.* It is traditional to be named for your paternal grandfather. Francesco, Matteo, Francesco, Matteo...'

'And your first son? Will he be Francesco?' she asked. Then, 'I'm sorry, I'm assuming you have no children already.'

'No children. I have never been married, Sarah.'

'Not even close?'

'I have never asked the question.'

Which didn't mean he hadn't considered it, she thought, but didn't press it.

'I read about your father,' she said, returning to her question. 'His death on the track. It was only when you said you'd come home when you were six that I made the connection.'

'It's impossible to keep a secret these days. Everything you want to know is available on the internet, at the press of a button,' he said wryly.

'Actually, it was the village I was interested in. Once I read that you lived in Turin I didn't follow it up. You told me that your mother took you home. Not what happened next.'

'No.' He looked at her. A long considering look, then said, 'My mother was in no state to do anything. She and my father had a terrible row the morning he was killed.'

'You heard them?' she asked, horrified.

'Everyone in the street heard them.'

She tried to imagine him as a small boy, listening to his parents fighting. How frightening that must have been.

'I'm so sorry.'

'It was a long time ago. My father was a playboy who'd had a string of affairs. He drove as he lived, Sarah. Recklessly. His machismo made him a hero, the darling of the gossip-writers. They adored him and my mother suffered a great deal of unkindness in the press—she should have been grateful to be his wife, not made such a fuss about him being a man, that sort of thing. When he died, they blamed her.'

'How cruel.'

'He was out of control in every area of his life, Sarah, but she loved him.'

'Of course. If she hadn't loved him she wouldn't have cared.'

'No. Thank you.' And, when she glanced up at him, 'So few people see that.'

'Poor woman.'

'It was relentless, Sarah. Terrifying. They

camped out on the doorstep until we became virtual prisoners. My mother was on the point of a breakdown by the time Nonna and my grandfather came to fetch us home. Once there, the village threw up a protective cordon. Any stranger was given short shrift. No one would give them the time of day, let alone a cup of coffee.'

'I got some curious looks myself.'

He smiled. 'I doubt that had anything to do with the fact that you were a stranger, *cara*.'

'Flattering, but you weren't there. They are still protective of you and your family. With good reason.'

'We are never going to make the tourist brochures that way.'

'Do you want to?'

'No.'

'A result. What happened to your mother, Matteo?'

'She recovered, resumed her modelling career, eventually remarried. Happily, I am glad to say. So often people repeat the same disastrous mistakes.'

'But you stayed with your Nonna?'

'My grandfather was still alive then. He insisted.' He glanced at her, catching her disbelief that his mother could have left him. 'My mother was never a country girl, Sarah, and she travelled a great deal.'

'I'm sorry. I'm doing it now. Judging her.'

'Unnatural wife, unnatural mother. They gave it to her with both barrels. Not that they would have approved if she'd dragged me around the world with her.'

'A lose-lose situation,' she agreed.

'She kept her head high, worked hard, kept away from the places where photographers hang out and eventually married Stephano's father. They're both in the fashion business, but so far behind the scenes that they don't make the papers.'

'And then it started again when Bella became famous,' she commented.

'Before then. They never forget. The minute I was old enough to be interesting I became a target.'

And a target for the kind of girls who wanted their photograph in the gossip magazines. He'd learned very early not to take adoration at face value. Until Katerina. 'I've had to live a very boring life to sink below their radar,' he said.

'It requires a serious threshold of boring for gossip magazines to lose interest. And I'm sure with Stephano in Rome under your care, life has its excitements.'

That, finally, tempted him to a smile. 'For "under my care", read all the benefits of home without parents around to cramp your style.'

'As I said, exciting.'

Matteo was, Sarah thought, very protective of his family. Not just of Stephano, but Bella, too. And it was easy to understand why he'd had his fill of intrusive journalists.

'Tell me something else,' she prompted. 'Something happy. Tell me about the first girl you fell in love with.'

'It's not the first girl that matters—' he hailed a passing cab '—but the last.'

'Tut-tut…' Then, 'I thought we were going to walk.'

'We can walk back.' He spoke to the driver and then joined her in the back of the cab.

'You are not going to get out of it that easily. This is an in-depth job interview,' she teased.

'You want references?' he asked, laughing. Job done. The cloud lifted from his face. His eyes lit up with amusement. 'Very well. The first girl I fell in love with was called Elena. She was a model. A six-foot goddess.'

'Why does that sound totally feasible?' she asked. He shrugged, all innocence, and she laughed. 'Okay, where did you meet her?'

'I'd gone to Milan to spend my fifteenth birthday with my mother. I called at the office. Elena got into the lift with me.'

'And?' she asked.

'She smiled at me and I damn nearly came in my pants.'

'Oh…' She tried not to laugh, but couldn't

help it, spluttering a desperate, 'I'm sorry,' from behind her hand, before she gave up and giggled.

'Now it's your turn.'

'My first love?'

'Not your first love. Your first kiss,' he demanded.

'Oh, no... Really?' she said.

'This is your game.'

'Is it? I thought you started it, but if you're quite sure? It's rather shocking,' she added.

'In that case, I want every detail,' he insisted.

'Okay. Well, it was at the school Christmas disco. I'd had a crush on Darren Michaels for months, but he was a year older than me so I was totally beneath his notice.'

'I find that hard to believe,' he murmured.

'I promise you. Anyway, in a desperate attempt to get his attention, to prove that I was totally cool and worthy, I let Ashley Carpenter kiss me under a bunch of plastic mistletoe he'd brought with him.'

'Plastic mistletoe?'

'It was a school disco. The real stuff was banned.'

'I sense this did not end well.'

'It was horrible—all clashing teeth and noses. I pushed him away with rather more force than necessary. He fell over and everyone laughed. I fled and Ashley, poor boy, turned tail and ran in the opposite direction whenever he saw me after that.'

'And Darren?'

'He hit puberty, developed acne and totally lost his charm.'

'Puberty? How old were you when all this happened?'

'Ten,' she admitted. 'I think it might have been the braces on our teeth that caused the problem. We were both wearing them and there was a certain amount of…entanglement.'

'I don't suppose there is a clip of this on the internet?' Matteo asked hopefully.

'Oh, please. Can you imagine the fun my students would have had with something like that?'

They were both laughing as the cab drew to a halt and Matteo helped her out.

'Where are we?' she asked, looking around.

'The one place in Rome that every visitor has to see.'

He took her hand, led her around a corner and there, before her, floodlit, was the vast marble edifice that was the Trevi Fountain.

Dozens of people were gathered around it, taking photographs, tossing in their coins.

'You did not have a photograph of it on your phone so I think perhaps you were not ready to make a commitment to Rome. That your heart was still in England with Tom.'

She swallowed. It was unnerving how easily he read her. But he was right, she had avoided this most famous of all Rome's monuments because, until now, Rome had been a place of exile. Despite its many attractions, it was a place to leave, not to come back to.

'You know the legend?' he asked.

'That if you throw a coin in the fountain you will return to Rome.'

He turned to her, drew her close, looking down into eyes. 'Do you want to return, Sarah?' he asked.

Right at that moment, with Matteo's arm around her waist, she never wanted to leave. She didn't say that. Like the kiss in her apartment, it was too intense for a first date. This was supposed to be light, fun and she said, 'Who would not want to return to Rome?'

'That was not what I asked, *cara.*'

'No…' A bit like his answer to the marriage question. It was an answer. But not the whole answer.

'Maybe you need more time to think about it,' he said, taking a step back.

'No!' He waited. 'I want to come back to Rome,' she said, with the emphasis on the 'I.'

Matteo nodded, reached into his pocket and produced a coin which he offered to her. Warm from his body. Warm from his fingers…

'Isn't that cheating?' she said. 'Shouldn't it be my own coin?'

'It works twice as well if the coin is given to you by your lover.'

'But we are not...'

'To make love is more than sex, Sarah. It is a journey of discovery and we have only just begun.' He took her hand, placed the coin in her palm, wrapping her fingers around it. Wrapping his fingers around hers. 'It has to be over your shoulder.'

'With my back to the fountain?'

He nodded, stepped back to give her room.

Never taking her eyes off Matteo, she raised the coin to her lips, then tossed it high over her shoulder.

'*Brava!* You reached the very heart of the fountain.'

'Is that good? Maybe I should do it again,' she said, suddenly anxious that it should work. 'Just to be on the safe side?'

He smiled as he leaned forward, kissed her cheek. 'Once is enough,' he said.

His breath was warm against her skin. His skin smelled faintly of something she could not pin down. A scent so subtle that it could not possibly have come out of a bottle. And he was right. Once was more than enough.

One look, one kiss, one touch...

'What happens to them all?' she asked,

glancing back as he took her hand and led her away from the throng of tourists. 'The coins.'

'They are removed by the city. Given to charity.'

They walked in silence towards the Piazza del Quirinale where the city, dominated by the dome of St Peter's, was spread out before them.

'Have you been to the Vatican?' he asked.

'Yes, but there's so much to see. I'll have to go back.'

'Wait until the tourists have gone. Another month and the city will be ours.' He glanced at her. 'You did not write about it in your blog.'

'There's a lot I don't put in my blog.' She looked up at him, remembering the furious tirade she'd written, finally deleted. Remembered wanting to be able to delete memories, feelings as easily.

Not this memory. This was one she would take out and treasure when she was old.

'Old Romans and churches?'

'Just going through the motions. No one is reading it.'

'Shame. I enjoyed Horatius.' Then, 'Not even Lex?'

'Not even my mother. I don't imagine either of them are likely to visit the school website.' And even if they did they wouldn't find it now. It was just between the two of them. A private connection. 'I was only doing it because the Head twisted my arm.'

He raised his eyebrows.

'Metaphorically,' she assured him. 'He was concerned that people would think he'd got rid of me so that he could have Tom back. The school has a great sporting record, largely thanks to him.'

'So this man is using your blog to protect his back.'

He sounded outraged on her behalf, a fact that made her heart beat rather faster. 'Spot on. If anyone raised the issue he could point to my blog and say that I was still involved with the school, my pupils. That I will be back next autumn.'

'But you won't be.'

'No,' she admitted.

'You must miss them. And your friends.'

'Of course, but not as much as I thought. I'm enjoying my job here.' She smiled. 'And after my last post the Head removed the link from the school website as not suitable for family viewing. I tend to wear my heart on my sleeve. I'd be absolutely no use as a female Machiavelli.'

'Machiavella... The pursuit of ambition without conscience.' He looked at her for what seemed like an eternity, then said, 'Be glad.' He lifted her hand to his lips. 'I have had the misfortune to know two such women. Both pretended love. One betrayed my family, the other betrayed me.'

'Matteo…' she gasped.

'I was a child when my nanny sold her story to the gossip magazines, but I was old enough to understand the results. I was wrenched away from everything I knew. Even my mother became a stranger.' He turned away. 'The other betrayal was more personal. She pretended love with such skill, such passion that I did not, could not believe the truth until she admitted it. Told me to my face what she had done.'

He turned, her hand in his, continued to walk, but she dug in, refused to move. 'What?' she demanded. He stopped. 'You can't leave it there. Tell me!'

'Tell you…' He lapsed into Italian, as if he could not say the words in any other language than his own and, even before he stopped, she slipped her arm through his and began to walk with him, knowing somehow that it was important to keep him moving.

'Tell me,' she repeated, when he'd run out of words, but softly this time. 'Tell me what she did to you.'

They were walking through a small park, an avenue of trees lit in a gauzy haze of green, past some vast Roman edifice.

'Compared to what was done to my mother,

it was nothing so very terrible,' he said at last. 'She sold photographs she'd taken at Bella's wedding. Not the big reception with film people, politicians, covered by a magazine paying a fee to charity for the privilege, but the ones she had taken at the private mass in the church at Isola del Serrone. At the party in the villa to which only family and the closest friends were invited. She had a camera built into a handbag that I had given her for her birthday.'

Family, friends and lovers. As his partner, this woman would have had access to everything.

'Why?' She could understand why someone might attempt to infiltrate the wedding. But to have a man like Matteo di Serrone love you and then betray him—and he had to have fallen in love or it wouldn't have hurt him so much—how much money would ever compensate for such a loss? 'Why would she do such a thing?'

'For a starring role in a film. She was an actress and the publishers of the magazine owned the film company.'

'I suppose the pictures must have been worth a great deal of money,' she commented.

'They put a picture of Bella and Nico at the altar on their front cover. A strap line which read, *The "Real" Wedding*. They produced five times their usual print run, sold out within hours and printed again.'

'Didn't the other magazine sue? I'm sure I read about a case where that happened.'

'They couldn't. They hadn't bought the rights to those pictures. And Bella chose not to.'

For him, she thought. To save him the pain.

'How long had you known her?'

'Katerina? A few months. I met her at a party that the film studio threw for Bella's engagement. I was—' he searched for a word '—entranced.'

'You were entranced—' she forced herself to repeat the words '—and someone saw an opportunity.'

'Who knows what came first? The egg or the chicken. She was lovely. I had a reputation as a man who found no reason to resist a pretty face. Does it make a difference?' he asked bitterly.

Was it better if she had deliberately set out to snare him or, despite whatever feeling she had for him, had been seduced by an offer too good to refuse? If he had given her a ring, would she have changed her mind?

'Did she get the part?' she asked.

'Yes. I'm told that she is very talented.'

'Maybe she would have got the part, anyway.' Could have had both fame and Matteo. Did this Katerina ever wonder about that? Or was she truly Machiavella and didn't care?

'It's a tough business. There are many actresses, few parts and the photographs did not matter. On the contrary. The combination of the public's outrage at the intrusion, their desperation to actually see the photographs and her dignified silence turned Bella into a national icon.' He managed a smile. 'Fortunately, no one did anything shocking, there were no fights, no one got drunk and fell in the pool. No one was hurt by them.'

'Except you.'

He didn't deny it. 'It was the realisation that every word, every kiss, every touch had been a lie.'

About to suggest that was unlikely, she thought better of it. No question, it was worse to be betrayed by someone who loved you.

'Thank you for telling me. At least I understand why you were so suspicious when I turned up just at that moment. When everyone thought Bella was at the villa,' she added. 'Bad timing.'

'No.' He lifted his arm over her head and wrapped it around her shoulders, so that she was closer. 'There was nothing wrong with your timing. Nothing at all.' He pressed his lips to her hair. 'Your arm goes around my waist,' he prompted.

'Matteo—'

'Shh…'

'But—'

'No more talking.'

They walked on through gardens, narrow streets, stopped at a café, leaning against the counter as they tossed back an espresso, putting off the moment when they would arrive at her front door. Not wanting the evening to end.

But end it must and not in the tear-your-clothes-off heat of its beginning.

Matteo had said that to make love was a journey of discovery. They had both stumbled on the road, been hurt to the quick. They needed time to learn about each other. Learn about themselves. Take time to enjoy the scenery.

They climbed the cobbled stepped street to her 'palazzo', the four flights of stairs to her front door.

He took her key, unlocked it, then took her hand and kissed her palm.

'Thank you for a truly memorable evening, Sarah. I will call you.'

When…

'*Grazie*, Matteo. *Buonanotte. Sogni dolci.*'

He smiled.

She had gone to the web to look for 'sweet dreams'. Had she got it wrong?

'*Sogni dolci*, Sarah,' he said, then took a step back and, with a final nod, took to the stairs.

She forced herself to close the door the

minute he was out of sight when what she wanted most in the entire world was to run to the railings, lean over like a besotted fifteen-year-old to catch every last glimpse of him, every sound until the street door shut behind him.

Not cool.

Instead, she leaned back against her own door, the just-kissed palm against her heart.

She'd had boyfriends.

She'd been in love with Tom.

But Matteo was the first man who had ever taken the time to make love to her.

Matteo hit the street in record time, stood against the wall, his legs shaking.

He'd forgotten this desperate want, the need for a woman who lit you up like fireworks at the harvest fiesta.

Slow... Slow down.

They had both lost something important, something that could not be replaced with meaningless sex.

He began to walk, striding out through the city, ignoring the passing cabs until he reached a square with a bar. He ordered espresso and a shot of grappa.

What would she be doing now?

Sitting on the tiniest terrace in Rome breathing in the scent of the lemon thyme he'd dug from Nonna's garden with his own hands? He pictured her there, wearing a white lace-trimmed nightdress—she would certainly wear a nightdress—brushing her hair. Pictured her lying in bed, her hair spread out across her pillow.

He tossed back the grappa.

CHAPTER NINE

ITALIAN FOR BEGINNERS

I finally made it to the Trevi Fountain tonight, tossed in a coin to ensure that I will return to Rome...

SARAH picked up the broken crocks, wrapped them in newspaper. Mopped the kitchen floor. Smoothed out the spicy vanilla-scented petals of the poor broken roses, cutting off their heads and tucking them into a bowl of water that she placed beside her bed.

She hung up her clothes. Reached up to turn on the shower, brought her wrist to her face as she caught again Matteo's elusive scent clinging to her skin where he'd touched her. Turned off the shower, wanting to sleep with that.

She cleaned her face, brushed her teeth, pulled on a knee-length T-shirt-style nightie with a teddy bear on the front.

Not exactly sexy.

Should she buy something sexier? In black.

No. Nothing that obvious.

White then. Long. With tiny shoe-string straps and a touch of lace at the hem.

No. Too much the bride.

Then, remembering the hunger of the kiss they'd shared in the kitchen, she smiled. There was no need to worry about nightwear. Like Marilyn Monroe, all she'd need to wear in bed was a touch of scent. A thought that banished any chance of sleep.

She took her netbook out onto the terrace and opened up her blog, reread what she'd written.

...I will return to Rome...

She sighed. This was supposed to be about life in Rome and it was, but it was no longer for her students. It had become a personal odyssey, a journey to discover herself.

Matteo gave me the coin, but wouldn't let me throw it until I was sure I wanted to come back. It was a special moment—letting go of the past, looking forward to a new future. But right now, I'm sure of only one thing. That the journey is the thing. That I have to take my time, enjoy the scenery, treasure the stops along the way.

She posted the blog, logged off, closed the shutters, slid into bed, not to sleep—her brain was still whirring from late-night espresso, the zinging excitement of something new—but to relive every single moment since she'd opened the door to Matteo di Serrone.

Every touch. Every smile. That dreadful moment when his English had deserted him. Their walk through the park while he'd told her about the woman who he had loved. Who had betrayed him.

She was asking a lot of a man who had been so badly hurt, she realised.

Or maybe she was giving him exactly what he needed. If she could make him feel good about himself, give him memories that would make him smile years from now, then they would both win.

Her phone, lying beside the bowl of roses, began to ring. It was late and for a moment her heart flipped over, certain that it was bad news. Then it flipped again as she saw who was calling.

'Matteo…'

'I said I would call you. You were not asleep?'

'No, I was not asleep. I was lying here thinking.'

'What were you thinking about, *cara*?'

'I was thinking that you never told me three things about yourself that I don't know.'

'I will tell you one thing tonight,' he said. 'To go with my comic opera title, I have a box. At the opera.'

She didn't answer. It was as if she'd been wading into a warm sea and suddenly stepped off a ledge, plunged out of her depth in the cold, dark water.

Who on earth did think she was, telling him what she wanted and expecting him to deliver?

He was Conte Matteo di Serrone. His father had been a racing driver. His cousin was a film star and the nearest anyone had come to a box at the opera in her family was her father's season ticket to Maybridge United Football Club.

'You say nothing,' he said eventually. 'You do not like opera?'

'I've never been to a live performance,' was the best she could come up with.

'But you have no objection in principle?'

'None,' she whispered. In principle.

'To *Tosca* in particular?'

'*Tosca*...' She tried to think which one that was. 'Doesn't she die?'

'It is opera, *carissima*. Someone always dies. Actually, in *Tosca* everyone dies. Do you think you can bear it? If I bring an extra handkerchief.' He waited. 'Sarah?'

'Sorry, I was just thinking about that scene in *Pretty Woman*. The one where Richard Gere took Julia Roberts to the opera and an old dowager asked her if she had enjoyed it.'

'I don't believe I have seen it.'

'You wouldn't. It's a girl movie. Cinderella is rescued by the prince. The bad guy gets the sack. The prince...'

'Yes?'

'The prince is rescued by Cinderella. No one dies.'

'An equal opportunity fairy tale with a happy ending. So? Did she? Enjoy the opera?'

'Yes, she...' She stopped. 'Is it formal?'

'Black tie but no tiaras.'

'That's just as well. When?'

'In a couple of weeks. I'll have to check the exact date. Or maybe you will be busy interviewing other prospective candidates for the job?'

'And miss out on an evening sobbing into your monogrammed handkerchief?' she teased.

'I don't have monogrammed handkerchiefs, but I'll see if I can find one of my grandfather's. He had the same initials. We'll have supper afterwards.'

'It sounds...' Very grand. A black-tie night at the opera followed by supper with a Conte was a long way from Friday night at the pub in Maybridge. A game of skittles or shove ha'penny. Fish and chips on the way home. Then, as she heard noises in the background, 'Where are you?'

'I'm not sure. I stopped at a bar for a shot of grappa.'

'Grappa?' She'd heard of it, but never tried it.

'It is wholly Italian. The distilled essence of the grape. The pips, the skin left over from the wine-making. You will taste it when you come to the vineyard.'

'Will I like it?' she asked, storing up the fact that he wanted her to return to Isola del Serrone, to his home, to be taken out and explored later. Reminding herself that this was an equal opportunities affair. That she intended to give him as much as he gave her.

'Who can say? But you should try everything once.'

'Matteo...'

'I called to tell you that I will be away for the rest of the week. I did not want you to think I was a here-today-gone-tomorrow lover.'

'I'm a hardworking teacher,' she reminded him. 'I can't be gallivanting out every night with the aristocracy.'

'Of course. I am chastened.'

She could hear the smile in his voice. 'You don't know the meaning of the word.'

'Maybe not,' he admitted, 'but you will be free on Friday evening?'

'Certo.'

'Grazie. I will see you then. Sweet dreams, amore mio.'

'Take care,' she said, but he had gone. He did that, she thought. Left her wanting more. A heck of a lot more.

It was as if a jolt of electricity had been fed into her emotional mains and jump-started a part of her that she hadn't even realised had shut down.

How long had her life been simply ticking over?

Idling…

She lay back against the pillow, the phone still clutched in her hand as if it was still connected to Matteo.

The opera?

At least he hadn't sprung it on her. She had plenty of time to think about what to wear. Formal for evening meant what exactly? Long? Maybe. Classy—definitely.

Nothing in her wardrobe fitted that description. Forstunately, classy, in Roman terms, meant timeless.

So far there had been no call for evening clothes of any kind, but it was clearly time for an investment.

Something simple. Black, obviously…

It would be expensive but so well made that, with care, she would be able to take it out of her wardrobe ten years from now and it would still look good. And she'd smile at the memory of the first time she wore it. At the memory of the man she had worn it for.

Matteo took the long way back to the palazzo, forcing his steps away from Sarah, even while his head was filled with the image of her lying in bed. Bare shoulders golden in the lamplight, hair spread loose across her pillow.

Slow down...

Slow. Down.

He walked beside the river, attempting to burn off the restless sexual energy flooding his system, that fizzed through his veins like new wine whenever he saw her. Talked to her. Thought about her.

It would once have given him a power rush. A sense of being invincible. An adrenalin charge that would have powered him through all-night stints in the laboratory with his mind crystal-clear. Answers coming before he'd even thought of the questions.

But right now he was feeling a lot more like that fifteen-year-old boy in the lift. Wanting everything, but not entirely sure what everything was.

A few days away from her, he reasoned, would be no bad thing. This was too fast. He distrusted the intoxicating rush of desire. This feeling of being out of control was too much like last time. And yet at the same time nothing like it.

It was like nothing he had ever felt before. Always, before, he'd known exactly what he wanted. This uncertainty, this doubt, was unknown territory.

Time to cool down, with several countries between them, was exactly what he needed.

So why did it feel like a lifetime until Friday?

Matteo texted her on Wednesday evening: 'I am in Paris. It's raining and I'm soaked to the skin. I wish you were here.'

Sarah texted back: 'I am in the bath. I'm soaked to the skin, too. Wish you were here?'

The reply was in Italian.

Her phrase book was no help. On Thursday morning, she texted him after her run: 'I'm marking twenty essays on the Cold War before I go to school. My head aches, my shoulders ache and my fingers ache. Would a shot of grappa help?'

'Not grappa, cara. You need someone to stroke your temples, massage your shoulders, bring you coffee and pastries. Someone to kiss your fingers while you work.'

'That would do it. So where are you?'

'In Madrid. Reading a hundred-page report before a climate-change conference.'

'And this evening?'

'Working on my own paper.'

'I wish I was there to rub your shoulders. Instead I've got a friend coming for supper.'

'Keep Friday free. On Saturday I have to fly to New York. But tomorrow, amore mio, I am all yours.'

Matteo was smiling as he tossed the phone on his desk. Perfect lover checking in, job done. But as he eased his own shoulders, picked up the paper he had been studying, the words refused to come into focus. It was Sarah's face he saw. Her quick smile. Her sense of humour, her tenderness that filled his heart.

What would it be like to have someone to travel with you? A lover. A friend. Someone to talk to, laugh with. Who would kiss away the ache, shut out the world at the end of the day.

A hand to reach for in the darkness. A new thought and a dangerous one. He pushed it away.

Sarah's first run had been to shake off a disturbed night but it had been all she needed to get back into the routine. By the end of the week she was back in her stride, her muscles stretched and toned, her heart rate slowed.

On Friday she stopped on her way back to pick up fruit for her breakfast and was juggling the bag so that she could unclip her keys from her pocket when she looked up and saw a pair of legs blocking her way.

So much for her heart rate. It went right through the roof and she hadn't moved a step.

'Matteo…'

'I had hoped to get back last night but here I am as promised with coffee and fresh pastries.'

Strands of her hair, where they'd worked out of the elastic band holding it back, were sticking to her face. She was slicked with sweat, no doubt steaming slightly in the cool of the stairwell.

Not the image a girl wanted to present to a man who sent her untranslatable texts.

Matteo, on the other hand, looked every inch the well-groomed Italian male as he rose to his feet, balancing the tray containing coffee, the box of pastries in one hand.

'A man bearing coffee and cake is always welcome,' she managed. 'Can you give me a couple of minutes for a shower?'

'You say the most provocative things, *cara.*'

'I say the most ordinary things,' she said as she unlocked the door, put the fruit she'd bought on the table. 'You choose to put a provocative spin on them. I won't be long.' Heavens above, but he was gorgeous and she wanted to touch him. Kiss him. Show him how pleased she was to see him. As she was hot and sweaty, she contented herself with being provocative and, with a grin, said, 'Help yourself to an apple.'

'Wait…'

'What?'

He lifted a strand of damp hair from her cheek, tucked it behind her ear and then he cradled her face in his hands.

'Matteo, I'm…'

'Wait,' he said. And then he kissed her. Slow, thoughtful, it was everything his last kiss had not been. Where that had been fire, this had a gradual all-the-time-in-the-world warmth that had her toes curling with pleasure. When he finally lifted his head, he said, 'We missed our hello.'

'So we did.'

And she kissed him back, hopefully getting the same response from some part of him. Although her kiss had further to go to reach his toes.

'Ciao, Matteo. *Buongiorno. Come sta? Felice di—*'

'Go,' he said, laughing. 'Or your coffee will be cold.'

Saying hello to Matteo could—if she were lucky—lead to a whole lifetime of cold coffee but she emerged from the shower in record time, her hair wrapped in a towel, wearing only a bathrobe. She couldn't wait to get dressed. Or maybe she didn't want to be dressed.

'I've got five minutes,' she said, joining him on the terrace. 'We have a regular staff meeting on Friday morning and I'm still too new to risk being late.'

'Ten minutes. My driver is waiting. I will give you a lift.'

'No.' Being delivered to school in a chauffeur-driven car would raise eyebrows. 'Thanks. But I'll walk fast.' He laughed, offered her a pastry.

'Oh, yum,' she said, choosing a *cornetto* filled with cream. 'You certainly know the way to a woman's heart.'

'A misspent youth has its advantages. Turn around.'

'But…'

'You have no time to waste on buts, *cara*.'

She continued to look at him, no buts, no maybes, no hesitation… She wanted to soak up the sight of him. Imprint his face on her memory. The slight kink in the straightness of his nose. A tiny scar, high on his right cheekbone. His scandalously thick dark lashes. The way his hair was struggling to break free from a ruthless cut and curl around his ear.

And for a moment he looked right back at her.

Shiny pink face. Lashes non-existent without the special mascara that, according to the adverts, was supposed to turn them into thick fur, but didn't. Every blemish revealed.

Why on earth couldn't she have waited another moment to slap on a touch of foundation, make a quick pass with the mascara wand, lipstick?

Because she couldn't wait. Waste precious time putting on a face. Because he'd seen her at her worst and there was no need for pretence.

And that was how you fell in love, she thought.

Not with a desperate, rip-your-clothes-off kiss when you were looking your best. How could you not love a man who kissed you when you were red-faced, sweaty and looked about as bad as you possibly could?

A pull-you-close, I'm-glad-to-see-you, I've-missed-you kiss.

Matteo made a swivelling motion with his hand and, without a word, she turned so that her back was to him, but she was still looking over her shoulder.

'What is this…?'

The words died in her throat as he eased the robe away from her neck to reveal her shoulders, settling his hands in the curve of her neck.

'Coffee, pastry and a shoulder rub,' he reminded her as he began to gently knead at muscles she had thought were relaxed.

She groaned with pleasure, pastry forgotten.

'Good?'

'I'll give you twenty-four hours to stop…'

And then his thumbs reached the base of her neck, working into the top of her spine, and she forgot about everything except the heat pooling low in her belly.

His breath against her skin as he placed just one moist kiss in the nape of her neck.

This was how you fell in love. Not in glamorous trips to the opera, but in quiet moments of intimacy. A caring gesture.

The idea should terrify her. This was so not what she wanted. The prescription had been for wild nights and hot sex. Something to remember when you were so old that only the cats listened to you.

A lover, not this precious sharing of five minutes at the beginning of the day.

'Until tonight, *cara*,' Matteo said, lifting her robe back into place.

'I don't think I can wait that long.'

His smile was slow. 'You cannot be late and I, too, have meetings.'

'More meetings?' He was tired, she thought. He'd been working long hours, travelling incessantly, had only just arrived back in Rome; tomorrow he was leaving for New York and yet he had taken the time to come and spend a few minutes with her. 'I thought you worked on your vines.'

'That was last week. And maybe, if I am lucky, the week after next.'

'And this week?' she asked. 'What have you been doing in Paris and Madrid?' Apart from getting soaked to the skin. Aching shoulders as he bent over reports. 'What will you be doing in New York?'

'Giving papers at conferences. Chairing discussions.'

'And today?'

'Catching up at the office. I've spent the last couple of years working with the FAO, the UN's Food and Agricultural Organisation. The world needs food more than it needs wine.'

The time scale was not lost on her. After Katerina's betrayal he had changed his life and she instinctively lifted her hand to his cheek. 'It needs your wine, too, *caro*.'

'Pleasure and beauty. Italy's gifts to the world.'

'Yes…'

Without a doubt. But the superficial image of the gossip magazines had missed the real Conte di Serrone.

He may have inherited a little of his father's wildness, but he carried the genes of his grandfather and great-grandfather. Men of principle, honour whose commitment to country, to community, ruled their lives. That was who he was.

'Have you been to the Monte Testaccio?' he

asked, shaking off the moment of darkness that clouded his brow. 'Perhaps you would like to go to a club this evening?'

'Another time.'

'You have something else in mind?'

'An early night?' She reached out, laid her hand against the faint roughness of his cheek. 'You are tired, *caro*.'

'Sei bellissima.' He took her hand, kissed the palm, placed it against his cheek. 'Will you have dinner with me?'

'Of course. But here. I will cook—'

'No. I want to sit with you. To be with you. I have no idea what time I will finish this evening, but I will send a car for you at seven.'

'You don't have to take me out, Matteo.'

'I am not. I am taking you home.'

He leaned in for a final brief kiss and a moment later the door closed behind him.

It was considerably longer before Sarah could persuade her legs to support her.

The driver who knocked on her door promptly at seven was the same man who'd driven her from Isola del Serrone. Not chance, she would have bet the cashmere coat she'd thrown over her shoulders. Unable to come himself, he'd made sure she would feel comfortable with someone she knew.

Or was she reading too much into it?

She mustn't read too much into it. This was not for life but for fun, she reminded herself.

The car was different, though. Not a film star limousine, nothing to draw unnecessary attention, just an anonymous grey Mercedes with untinted windows which, having negotiated the Rome traffic, drew up in a narrow street in front of a pair of impressive doors.

The driver rang the doorbell and waited until it was opened by a middle-aged woman.

'Signora Gratton?' A middle-aged woman regarded her for a moment, then smiled. *'Benvenuta.'*

'Grazie.'

The hallway she stepped into was stunning and, remembering how she'd dismissed the idea that Matteo might actually live in a genuine palazzo as nonsense, she felt rather stupid.

'Io sono Anna… I am the Conte's housekeeper,' she added carefully. 'He is…*fare il bagno.'*

In the bathroom… 'Taking a shower?' she ventured.

Anna smiled. *'Si!* He is in the shower. *Una momenta.'* She took her coat. *'Vuole qualcosa de bere?'*

'No, Grazie.' What was Italian for I will wait? *'Vorrei…'* I would like… She had been in Italy for weeks—she should be doing better

than this. '*Vorrei*...to wait for Matteo. The Conte,' she added quickly.

Anna nodded, indicated a formal sitting room where, with a mixture of Italian, English and many gestures, she invited her to make herself comfortable. Sarah, more interested in a Roman mosaic mounted behind a glass panel in the hall, abandoned her tote on the nearest chair and went back to take a closer look.

'It's the real thing.'

She spun around to see Matteo descending the stairs, casually dressed in a pair of chinos, a black polo shirt. Hair still damp from the shower.

'This place was built on the remains of a Roman villa. The tesserae were found in the basement when the plumbing threw in the towel a few years back.'

'I'll bet that slowed down replacing the pipework.'

'Just a bit,' he agreed with a rueful smile. 'I shouldn't have made the archaeologists so comfortable. Would you like to look around?'

'Please.'

They toured the house. On the ground floor there was the formal sitting room, a vast dining room filled with portraits of long dead Contes and their Contessas. A library filled with leather-covered volumes that were no doubt worth a fortune.

On the first floor there was a large sitting room with a television, more books, but mostly modern paperbacks this time, and comfortable furniture with no pretensions to grandeur.

'This is what my mother would call a "feet up" room,' she said.

'Good name. My brother puts his feet up in here all the time.'

'Does he live with you?'

'No. He has an apartment, but his mother is in Milan so he comes here when he wants to eat, or someone to do his laundry.'

'Students...'

'He crossed a wide hall to a room where the desk, the computer, filing cabinets told their own story. 'This is my office. It's where your postcard was lost in a pile of mail for an entire week,' Matteo said. He picked up the heap that had arrived while he had been away by way of demonstration.

'I gave it to the driver. I still can't believe I had the nerve,' she admitted, still brought to a blush at the thought of her saucy PS.

He lifted a hand to her cheek, stroking it lightly with the back of his fingers. 'I would have come to find you in your schoolroom if you had not sent it.'

'Would you?'

'I could not get you out of my mind.'

'That makes two of us,' she said. No pretence.

Then, because it was all much too intense, she said, 'Is there any chance you could teach me a few useful phrases over supper? Pippa, the school secretary, wanted to come around tonight and I'm afraid I told her a big fat lie about starting Italian lessons.'

'Because you don't wish to be gossiped about?'

'No, Matteo. Because I don't want you to be gossiped about.'

He seemed about to say something but instead took her hand. 'A few useful phrases? Very well. Say after me— *Voglio tenere voi.*'

'Voglio tenere voi?'

'It is not a question, *carissima*, it is a declaration. To be said with all your heart. Try again.'

She gave it another go, fairly sure that this was not something along the lines of *Please can you tell me the way to the railway station.*

'Perfetto,' he said, and he put his arms around her, drew her close, holding her against him so that her head was on his shoulder and she could feel his pulse.

'Now say— *Voglio baciare si...*'

He said the words softly, tenderly and when she lifted her head and repeated them her reward was a long, slow kiss.

Her hands looped around his neck, she

leaned back and looked up at him. 'This is the say-and-do lesson plan?'

'Simple but effective. Will you sign up for the whole course, do you think?'

'I'm liking it very much so far. What comes next?'

'Voglio fare l'amore con te...'

She repeated the words but he did nothing, said nothing, just looked at her with an intensity that sent a shiver through her.

'What did I just say, Matteo?'

'I want to make love with you...'

'And do you?' she whispered.

'Do you doubt it? Perhaps I'm not the hot lover that you were looking for, *amore mio.*'

'No?'

'Always away. Always busy.'

He turned away, but she reached up, took his face in her hands and made him look at her.

'Everything you do is more than I was looking for, Matteo. This morning, when I saw you waiting at my door...' She stopped. She had no words to describe how she'd felt when she'd seen him there. Not without using that terrifying four-letter word that he hadn't signed up for. That she hadn't signed up for. But she'd carried the warmth of it, the joy of it with her all through the day. 'Our journey may be slow but it is infinitely enjoyable. And the scenery is spectacular.'

He raised an eyebrow. The corner of his mouth tucked up into a smile. 'Please. Don't stop.'

'You said it. If all I wanted was sex I could have gone to the Testaccio any night of the week, taken a quick flight to nowhere.'

'Instead of which you are...?' he prompted.

'Taking a trip on the Orient Express. First class. Stopping at every station to explore.'

'What happens when the train eventually arrives in Venice?' he asked.

'Whatever we want. Kiss goodbye and move on with a pocketful of memories to take out and smile over when we're old,' she suggested.

'And if we don't want it to end?'

'We could turn around and go back. Do it all over again.'

'Better to travel on. We could charter a sailing ship and explore the Mediterranean,' he offered. 'Let the wind blow us where it will.'

'You see how easy it is,' she said. 'Beauty and pleasure. No stress. Taking it one stop at a time.'

'That's what you said on your blog.'

'You read it?'

'Do you want me to stop?'

She swallowed hard. 'You are on the journey with me, Matteo...' Then, 'Weren't you showing me your house?'

'There are two more floors, a dozen more

rooms, but they will keep. Come, I want to show you my favourite place.'

He led her back downstairs, through the formal sitting room towards French windows that stood open to a sunken, colonnaded court-yard.

From the outside no one would ever have guessed that there could be such a quiet, pri-vate space in the heart of the city.

A stone burble fountain made from an old grindstone stood at its heart. Overgrown with ferns and mosses, an amphora lying on its side at the base, it looked as if it had been there for centuries. Perhaps it had.

She crossed ancient, worn paving slabs, bent to let the water trickle over her fingers.

'Someone suggested I should install con-cealed lighting,' Matteo said, standing back to watch her.

'Really? I'd much rather sit out here with the light fading, listening to the sound of the water,' she said, refusing to ask who had sug-gested it, to think about who had suggested it, preferring to concentrate on the fact that he had not done it. 'This place is timeless.' Then, smil-ing up at him, 'If you were wearing a toga, we could be in ancient Rome.'

'Lying on a marble bench, eating grapes?' He shook his head as he joined her. 'I think we'd both be more comfortable on a chair.'

A table had been laid in the corner, a votive candle flickered as they disturbed the air, sat down.

They ate slowly, taking their time, talking about nothing much. Their week, their day.

Matteo found himself telling her what he would be doing in New York. His work on the development of salt-water tolerant plant strains. About the harvest, soon to begin in Isola del Serrone. First the grapes then, in November, the olives.

'You will come?' he asked.

'To help with the harvest? Or is it mechanised?'

Not to watch, he noted, but to help.

'We don't crush the grapes with our feet these days,' he said, and if he was smiling it was not because he was laughing at her, but delighted with her. 'They are, however, still cut by hand just as they were in the time of the Caesars. Everyone joins in.'

'I will be honoured to be a part of that, Matteo.'

Honoured...

She had the gift of choosing exactly the right word as naturally as breathing, he thought. They honoured the vines for what they gave them, blessed them, thanked God for the harvest and celebrated it with fireworks and feasting.

There was a simple joy in it. The same feeling he had when he thought of Sarah, talked to her, was with her. He had thought to offer her himself as a gift, but he was the one enriched by her presence. Would be the poorer when, heart-whole, she returned home.

The thought was so painful that he finally surrendered to the truth.

'It is late,' he said, 'but I cannot bear to let you go.' He reached for her hand, raised it to his lips. 'Will you stay with me tonight, Sarah? Be here when I wake up. Be the last thing I see before I leave for New York in the morning.'

CHAPTER TEN

ITALIAN FOR BEGINNERS

I was a guest at a Roman palazzo this weekend. Not a house divided into apartments or a purpose-built block of flats.

A palace built on Roman foundations.

Four storeys, two dozen rooms, a central courtyard with a fountain and a resident Conte. The real deal.

And I'm making progress with my Italian. I'm no longer a beginner.

MATTEO stirred as the sunlight slanted through the bars of the shutters. Opened his eyes. Sarah was curled up against him within the circle of his arm, her hand on his waist as if to keep him from slipping away before she woke.

No chance of that.

From the moment he had seen her sitting in the sunshine on the crumbling wall above his house, had kissed her, he had been lost. Even while he was telling himself that he was in control, that it was all a game, he had been fooling himself.

He was not Katerina.

He could no more make love to a woman he did not care for than Sarah could go to a nightclub and pick up a man to share her bed. He was long past the age where sex without commitment had any appeal.

He touched her cheek, his fingers tracing the gentle curve of her cheek.

'Voglio rimanere qui con voi,' he murmured as he continued along the line of her jaw. She stirred, leaning into his touch, her hair sliding against his chest.

There had been a moment last night when he had pulled a pin from her hair and it had cascaded over her naked shoulders. Her skin had been silvered by the moon and words had, for once, forsaken him.

He had forgotten this wonder. The slow unfolding, the complete surrender, the gift of yourself.

'I am falling in love with you,' he said, repeating the words in English.

The backs of his fingers traced the profile of her chin, her neck, the soft swell of her breasts as if committing them to memory.

'Voglio stare con te per sempre...'

'Mmm?' Sarah opened her eyes, looked up, smiled, said 'Ciao.'

'Ciao, *carissima*.'

'Voglio stare con te per sempre...' She repeated his words perfectly. 'What does it mean?'

'You should not listen to a man talking to himself.'

'That bad?' she said, but she was smiling up at him.

'Roughly translated, it means that I do not want to get up,' he said. *I want to stay with you forever*...left him far too exposed.

'I thought it might be something like that. I could come to the airport with you,' she offered.

'No,' he said, gathering her close. 'I want to remember you just like this. Naked. In my bed.'

ITALIAN FOR BEGINNERS

I have been invited to the opera. Just saying. I wouldn't want you to think that I was spending all my time shopping, eating ice cream and having fun in bed with my red-hot Italian lover.

Having been booted off the school website, she was now utterly free to write exactly what she wanted, knowing that only Matteo would read it. That, halfway across the world, in the midst of all the serious stuff, she could make him smile. Make him hot.

> *Not that culture isn't fun, although I am going to see Tosca, in which, I'm reliably informed, everyone dies.*
>
> *The upside, obviously, is that I have to buy a new dress. And shoes with very high heels. The stockings I bought are so fine that they are no more than a shimmer on my skin and that was before I got started on underwear. I didn't know they still made those all-in-one things in black lace with hooks up the back. Like something out of a sexy historical romp. Lots and lots of hooks.*

Matteo called her every evening. Sent her texts in Italian, which were—mostly—translatable. With the help of the new dictionary she'd bought.

Her replies made Matteo laugh a lot, presumably because she made so many mistakes but, although she'd signed up for Italian lessons, she could hardly ask her teacher for help translating her naughty little texts.

He had suggested she read an article in an Italian newspaper every day to help with her vocabulary and she'd stopped at a kiosk on her way to work to pick up a paper. The latest gossip magazines were piled high and on the cover of one the name 'Isabella' was splashed across a photograph of a woman wearing dark glasses, a scarf draped around dark hair, a black coat over her shoulders.

The broken heart and question mark didn't need a dictionary and she easily resisted the temptation to buy a copy. It was the magazine that had published the stolen pictures and she had no doubt that whatever they'd written was no more than speculation. At least she hoped it was.

She knew how worried Matteo was about Bella and her husband. Knew the damage that could be caused by unfounded gossip.

And then on Friday morning, when she came back from her run, he was there, sitting at the top of the stairs, waiting for her.

She hadn't been expecting him until the following morning, but she didn't bother to ask him why he was a day early. She didn't waste time talking, just grabbed his hand and, shedding clothes as she went, hauled him into the shower with her. Only then did she say, 'Hello.'

She came home at four to find that he'd left a gift for her on the small table by the sofa. A small blue carrier containing a blue box tied with a white ribbon. Inside the box was a soft blue case and, inside that, nestled a pair of ear-

rings. Long polished slender spirals of silver...
No, not silver. White gold.

She had her phone in her hand to call him as
she walked into her bedroom to try on the earrings.

No need. Face down in a pillow, broad naked
back gleaming in the evening sunlight, every
muscle and sinew totally relaxed, he was fast
asleep in her bed. But for the earrings in her
hand, the fact that at some time during the day
he'd picked up his scattered clothes, he might
not have moved since she'd left him that morning to go to school.

She quietly placed the earrings and the phone
on the dressing table, stepped out of her clothes
and slipped in beside him.

They left Rome early on Saturday, while the
sky was still pink, heading for the vineyard at
Isola del Serrone.

'Your Nonna won't mind?' Sarah asked a
touch nervously.

'Why should she mind?'

She lifted her shoulders, made a tiny awkward gesture and he reached out, caught her
hand, without taking his eyes from the road.
'You have my word that she will not mind me
bringing home a beautiful girl.'

'You've done it before?'

'She won't mind,' he said, 'because this is

the family home and you will be sleeping on your own in the guest room.'

'Oh.'

'Wish you'd stayed in bed for another hour, *cara*?'

She laughed. 'Don't you?'

'You were so eager to be away…' He glanced at her. 'Maybe we should take a walk on the path above the house,' he suggested. 'Try a rerun of that kiss.'

'Make love in the grass?'

'Is that what you felt?' She looked at him. 'You certainly felt something.'

'I felt… The grass was soft, green…'

'Spring grass?'

'He kissed her and they made love one last time before he went to the waiting Jeep, flew home to his wife and a baby son he'd never seen.'

'It was war, *cara*. They took comfort where they found it and lived every day as if it was their last.' His hand remained on hers, a gentle, reassuring presence, until they reached a junction and he had to change gears. 'She saw you, Nonna, that first morning when you came to the village,' he said as they approached the village. 'You went into the church?'

'I was going to talk to the priest. I thought he would be the best person to ask about Lucia. But he was busy.'

'So you decided to take a walk up the hill.'

She shook off the shadow of the past and smiled at him. 'It was a good move.'

'I'm glad you think so. Actually, it occurred to me that Nonna should be able to tell you more about Lucia. She was younger, of course, but she might remember something. Or have heard some gossip at the time. I can't believe that no one knew that she was hiding your great-grandfather.'

In the event what Nonna knew, or didn't know, never arose. Graziella met them with the news that the Contessa had gone to Naples to visit a cousin who was in the hospital and wouldn't be back before Monday.

'Do you want to go and see her too?' Sarah asked. 'I know how strong family ties are in Italy.'

He shook his head. 'Nonna was my great-grandfather's second wife,' he explained. 'She's Bella's grandmother, but her only relationship to me is through love.'

'The men in your family seem to inspire devotion,' she said. And instantly regretted it.

But Matteo was grinning. 'Come and have some breakfast. Put something other than your foot in that pretty mouth.'

Tractors and trailers were lined up in the vineyard, the priest blessed the vines, Matteo cut the first bunch of golden grapes. Then it began. Sarah took the plastic bucket she was offered, a pair of secateurs and pitched in alongside Matteo, piling the grapes into the trailer.

'I'm going up to the plant,' he said after a while, taking the secateurs from her and handing them to someone else. 'Come and see what happens next.'

Women were sorting the grapes as they were tipped onto a conveyor, through a machine that removed the grapes from the stalks, before being crushed.

Then, as she eased her back, he said, 'Do you want to see the caves where the wine is matured?'

'Heavens,' she said as she saw row upon row of vast wooden barrels. I had no idea...' She stopped as, out of sight of everyone, he began to massage her back, easing the ache. 'Oh, yes!'

'Better?'

'I feel a total wuss. Everyone else will be working all day.'

'They are used to it. Besides, I've been wanting to do this,' he said as he backed her into a bay housing one of the barrels and kissed her. 'And this,' he said, sliding his hands inside her T-shirt to unclasp her bra. 'And this.'

She leaned back over the gentle curve of the barrel, sighing with pleasure as he took possession of her breasts. 'Is this what is known as being had "over a barrel"?'

He shook his head, clearly not familiar with the expression.

'At your mercy, my lord,' she explained.

'On the contrary, *cara*, I rather think that I am at yours.'

The day passed in something of a blur. Only Sarah seemed to be in focus, at the centre of everything. She had slipped into the fabric of his world. Concentrating as she'd cut her first grapes. Attempting to communicate with the village women who'd come to help with the harvest, using gestures where words failed her.

Her eyes shining in the dim recesses of the cave, lighting up his life, making him believe.

They swam in the pool before breakfast, toured his laboratories, the nursery where he was growing new vines, looked in on the harvest.

'I feel guilty,' Sarah said as he picked a rose from one of the bushes that were planted at the end of each row of vines and handed it to her. 'I'm sure if I wasn't here you'd be working too.'

'We're just a distraction. Come on, I'll introduce you to Nonna's bees.'

'Matteo…' She hung back. 'That's very personal.'

'They're family. I understand. But they've

already taken a good long look at you,' he said, surrendering himself utterly to this woman who had wandered into his life and turned it on its head. 'It is only polite to return the visit. And afterwards we'll walk down to the church and light a candle for Lucia.'

'This plaque was erected by Matteo di Serrone in blessed memory of his foster mother Lucia Rosa Mancini, wife of Roberto Leone. At rest in the arms of Mary. 1898—1944.'

Matteo translated the plaque for her, and then they both lit a candle, sat for a while in silence remembering the woman who had saved the life of Matteo's grandfather by suckling him as a baby.

Finally, Matteo said, 'It isn't her, is it? Your Lucia.'

'No.'

The dates weren't right. According to Lex, she'd be in her eighties. Even if he'd got that wrong, or she'd been inventive with her age because he was younger than her, it still wouldn't account for the difference.

'I shouldn't have leapt to conclusions. It was just her connection with the family, the house. I'm sorry,' he apologised.

'Don't be.'

'I don't know where to begin to look. Every girl is named after someone else in her family. A grandmother, an aunt. There could be half a dozen Lucias in one generation of the same family. Nonna is Rosa Lucia after her grandmother and a cousin.'

'Pretty name.'

'Maybe she will be able to help.'

'No,' she said quickly. 'Let the past lie, Matteo.'

'More Italian lessons tonight?' Pippa asked as Sarah dropped off some papers in the office on Friday evening.

She should have told her she was dating Matteo. Driving out of Rome to eat at little restaurants in the country where no one knew him. Evenings in his palazzo. But it would be all over the school in ten minutes—Pippa couldn't keep a secret to save her life.

She wanted to keep what they had private for as long as possible. Private, if you didn't count the entire population of Isola del Serrone, but they were people who knew how to keep a secret.

'That's me,' she said. 'A glutton for punishment. You?'

'I'm going home for the weekend, but I've got something for you.' She scrabbled around in her bag, produced a memory stick and tossed it to her.

'What's this?'

'A copy of all the Lucia stuff Federico dug up on that genealogy site. Birth, marriage and death certificates, that sort of thing. I know you didn't want him to go on and I did tell him, but once he's got his teeth into something...' She shrugged. 'Anyway, I downloaded it from his computer. Just in case you change your mind. It'll need translating. Good practice for you.'

'Downloaded?' Then, realising just how bad Pippa looked, she forgot her hurry, pulled up a chair, sat down. 'What's wrong?'

'Nothing.' Pippa shrugged. 'If you don't count all the secret lunches, the afternoons who knows where, Federico has been spending with another woman.'

No... 'Are you sure?'

'Absolutely. It's been obvious he's up to something so I read his emails. Only a man would be stupid enough to use the name of his football team as a password.'

She pulled a face that was supposed to be comic, but the tear sliding down her cheek ruined the effect. '"Meet me in the usual place" emails. All initials.'

'But...he seems devoted to you, Pippa.' All kisses, hand-holding, smiles. 'Have you talked to him?'

'He's been a bit hard to get hold of this week. You know...*busy*.'

'Oh, Pippa...'

'I left a message on his voicemail telling him to pick up his stuff. Then I spotted that folder and copied it onto a memory stick before I tossed the cheating scumbag's laptop out of the window along with the rest of his belongings. Which is why I'm going home for the weekend. In fact, that's my taxi now.'

Sarah had never spent so much money on so little dress, but missing Matteo, she had decided to distract herself with a little shopping and, braving one of the designer shops in the Via dei Condotti, she explained to the scarily elegant woman who had approached her what she was looking for.

Something classic for evening.

In black.

'Black is always safe,' she had agreed.

Something about the woman's response suggested that 'safe' was not something of which she approved. In fact, translated, she clearly meant 'boring'.

'No,' she replied firmly. '*Classic.* Like Audrey Hepburn.' No one could say she was boring.

The woman sighed. 'Of course. You and every other woman.'

What was this? She'd come into the shop to spend her very hard-earned money on designer clobber and she was being patronised by the sales woman?

On the other hand, it was true that, however much she paid for an LBD, she was never going to look like the gorgeous Audrey. And she didn't want to look like every other woman out for a night at the opera.

She was making memories, not just for herself but for Matteo, and she wanted him to remember how she looked as vividly as Lex remembered Lucia.

In the end she did choose something in black. Depending on which way you looked at it. Shot silk taffeta, it was black this way, a dark teal-green the other way.

The off-the-shoulder bodice fitted like a glove, the tiny straight skirt covered maybe half her thighs and a wide black chiffon sash trailed foot-wide ribbons behind her almost to the floor. Definitely not the kind of safely classic dress that she'd be able to take out of the wardrobe and wear ten years from now at a 'bit of a do'.

She had rolled her hair into a loose coil at her neck, was wearing stockings that were no more than a shimmer. High heels that were probably suicidal on those cobbles.

As a finishing touch, she had added Matteo's

earrings, which were so long that they dropped nearly to her shoulder.

Simple. Absolutely. In the manner of scream-out-loud, look-at-me simple.

What on earth had *possessed* her?

A tap on the door at precisely seven o'clock provided the answer.

For Matteo.

For that look as his eyes swept from her head to her feet and then back up again until he met her own.

For that smile.

'I fear I may have lost the power of speech,' he said eventually.

'On the contrary, you have said exactly the right thing. And while I will freely admit that your brother is very pretty, he has a lot of growing up to do before he can begin to compete with you.'

Nothing showy. Just good tailoring, the simplest pleated dress shirt, a hand-tied bow tie. Wide shoulders, a face bone-deep with character, dark eyes that seemed to generate heat, warm her.

'Do you have a coat?'

'Is it cold?' she asked.

'No, but there are some boys in the street who are nowhere near old enough for the ideas that dress will give them.'

'You would deprive them of your own formative experiences?'

'Absolutely. And it will be chilly later.'

She fetched her coat. He put it around her shoulders, took her hand and they walked in silence down the hill to the chauffeur-driven car waiting on the roadside. The driver opened the door as they approached and she stepped in, feeling rather like a princess, although she had the sense not to say so.

There were crowds outside the Opera House. People turned to look at her as Matteo handed her from the car. Several people called out to him, but he merely nodded or raised a hand in acknowledgement and kept going.

'Matteo, if you want to stop and talk, I don't mind,' she said.

'The only person I want to talk to tonight is you.'

A member of the front of house staff greeted him warmly. Champagne was offered. They both refused it. A heavily embossed programme was produced and presented to her with a slight bow.

'Signora.'

'Grazie.'

Inside the theatre, rows of gilded boxes rose from floor to ceiling around an auditorium filled with the buzz of expectancy. Below them, the orchestra was tuning up.

'How is it so far?' he asked.

'Amazing.' Forget the opera, the fabulous theatre, none of that mattered. Just being with him was... 'Absolutely amazing.'

The lights dimmed, the overture began and behind them, the door of the box opened and a couple slipped into seats on the far side of Matteo, murmuring their apologies.

He leaned close, whispered, 'My cousin and her husband. I'm sorry, I had no idea they were coming tonight. I'll introduce you in the interval.'

She leaned forward to acknowledge their arrival but, since they appeared to be conducting an argument sotto voce, neither of them noticed her. She exchanged a wry glance with Matteo, then turned her attention to the stage and let the power and passion of the opera sweep over her.

'Well?' Matteo murmured as the first act came to a close. 'Did you?'

'What?'

'Nearly 'pee your pants'.'

She let out something between a gasp and a laugh. 'Are you telling me that you sat through a "girl" movie simply to find out what Julia Roberts said?'

'I have to confess that I asked my secretary.' He continued to look at her for a moment before he said, 'Sarah, may I introduce my cousin,

Isabella di Serrone, and her husband, Nico Bazzacco. Bella, Nico, Sarah Gratton.'

'Sarah of the cryptic postcard!' Bella exclaimed. 'I'm so sorry for intruding on your evening but Nico arrived home this morning and—'

'—and you thought you'd put in a public appearance to demonstrate the fact,' Matteo said, cutting her short.

'—*and*,' she continued, 'it's his favourite opera.'

'It's your favourite opera,' her husband muttered. 'Give me Verdi every time.'

'Behave, children, or I'll have you thrown out of my box and that will certainly ensure that you make tomorrow's front page. For all the wrong reasons,' he added.

Sarah was only dimly aware of the bickering between the star and her husband. The theatre, the noise of the crowds, even Matteo faded into the background. Only Isabella di Serrone was in focus.

Her hair, a mass of dark glossy curls, tumbled about her shoulders and Angelo had not exaggerated her smile, but it was her eyes, huge, liquid, almost black in the low lighting of the theatre, that brought her heart to her throat.

She knew those eyes. Had seen that smile on the torn photograph that her great-grandfather had kept for more than sixty years.

She was looking at Lucia, but not wartime skinny in a faded cotton frock, sitting on a wall in the June sunshine. This was Lucia well-fed, pampered, make-up perfect, jewels at her throat. Dressed in the finest fashion that Milan could offer.

Clearly she was used to reducing people to silence because the fact that Sarah hadn't said a word or made the slightest move didn't appear to faze her. She shooed Matteo out of his chair and moved into it.

'You are a teacher, I think.'

'Yes...' Her mouth formed the word but no sound emerged.

'Matteo told me that you met in Isola del Serrone.' She paused, expecting some response.

Dimly, in her head she registered the fact that Matteo had talked about her to his family.

'Is our little village going to be the new tourist hotspot?' Bella prompted.

Matteo, who'd been talking to Nico, came to her rescue. 'Sarah's great-grandfather was there during the war, Bella. A local woman saved his life. Hid him for months.'

'How romantic! Were you hoping to trace her?

Trace her...

She was standing right in front of her.

'She should talk to Nonna, Matteo. She's lived in the village all her life. Nico, darling,

it's like a movie. In fact, it could be a movie…'
She turned to her husband and, forgetting their
tiff, began to speak in rapid Italian, no doubt
telling him the story.

'I'm sorry about this circus, Sarah,' Matteo
said. 'If I'd known…' Then, 'Are you all right?'

'I'm fine.'

'You look a little pale.'

'Do I?' Well, that was hardly surprising.
Seeing a grainy old photograph come to 3D full
colour life in front of you would take the wind
out of anyone's sails. 'I'm a bit warm. Perhaps a
glass of water?' she suggested.

There was a tray of drinks, glasses on a
small table at the rear of the box and he opened
a bottle of water, handed her a glass. 'We don't
have to stay.'

'You're suggesting we leave before I find
out if Tosca can persuade the horrible Chief of
Police to pardon her lover? I don't think so.'

He said nothing. Instead he reached into
his pocket and produced a soft white monogrammed handkerchief and placed it in her
hand.

She didn't cry. The drama was too intense,
the ending inevitable. It was beyond tears.

Bella and Nico left in a round of kisses, but
Matteo held her back.

'Someone will have called in the news that
Bella is here and the front entrance will be

knee-deep in photographers,' he said, calling his driver and heading for a side exit.

Even from there, the scrum was visible as the paparazzi crowded in for close-ups.

'Are all the women in your family so beautiful?' she asked.

'There aren't many,' he said. 'No one else of that generation. I can't remember her mother at that age, although photographs don't suggest that she had that star quality. She was in her late forties when Bella was born. Bella was totally spoilt, of course.'

'And you were not? I thought all Italian boys are spoilt as a matter of course.'

'Nonna tends to the tough love school of child-rearing. Maybe if my grandmother had lived I'd have been as much of a brat as Stephano.'

It was like a cog dropping into place. A spinning gear catching, the engine moving smoothly on. Nonna was Bella's grandmother. Nonna—Rosa Lucia—was the girl in the photograph.

Sarah wanted to shout out, grab him, tell him, but it was a secret that his Nonna had kept for more than sixty years. And she'd seen Sarah in the church. Recognised something familiar.

Had she known? Been afraid that her secret would be revealed. Had she made an excuse to go away last weekend to avoid meeting her, no doubt hoping that it was no more than a passing fancy? That Matteo would soon tire of her. Move on...

She had to see her, talk to her, tell her that her secret was safe with her. That no one would ever hear it from her.

It wasn't as if Lex was waiting for news. He'd told her to leave it.

She had only wanted to know that if Lucia was still alive, she was in a good place. Which she was. She'd married a Conte. Lived in that beautiful villa. Had a daughter, a granddaughter. Was dearly loved—not least by Matteo.

'Why are you smiling?' Matteo asked.

'Nothing.' She leaned against him, her head on his shoulder. 'I was just thinking how dull my family seem by comparison.'

'Except for your great-grandfather and his Italian adventure.'

'Except for that,' she agreed. Then, looking up at him, 'How hungry are you?'

'That depends what we're talking about.'

'I'm talking about going home, right now,' she said, suddenly desperate to hold him, to be held. 'Your place or mine?'

Matteo pulled a face. 'I have a sinking feeling that Bella and Nico plan to stay at the palazzo tonight. Happy or fighting, they tend to be noisy and I don't want any distractions when I'm undoing all those hooks,' he said, running his thumb down her spine in a way that made her forget all about Bella, Lucia and pretty much everything else.

'Have you been reading my blog again?' she asked.

He grinned. 'Why else would you be writing it?'

Some nights would live in the mind for ever and this was one of them. It seemed endless, as if time was stretching out just for them, their senses heightened so that every touch, every kiss, every part of love was brand new.

They got up, starving, in the middle of the night, made scrambled eggs and toast, and ate it on the terrace with the city asleep at their feet.

Then, chilled, ran back to bed and clung to each other, laughing at nothing, at everything, falling asleep as dawn turned the sky pink.

When Sarah woke it was late and she was alone. Matteo had propped a note beside the bed:

Al mio amore—*I have gone home to change. Pack an overnight bag and I'll pick you up at two. I want you to meet Nonna.* Siete la mia aria—*M.'*

To my darling—
You are my air—

She held the note to her cheek.

Siete la mia aria...

'Matteo...'

He'd showered, changed, was on his way out when Nico appeared at the sitting room door. 'Can it wait?'

'I'm afraid not.'

He sighed and, anticipating more marital disharmony, crossed to the sitting room. Bella was sitting, white-faced, in the corner of the sofa, unable to look at him.

'What is it? I thought you two—'

'This isn't about us.'

Nico held out the latest copy of his least favourite gossip magazine. The cover photograph was one that had been taken at Bella's wedding. Nonna, Bella's mother, Bella.

The strap-line read: *Secrets of the Serrones.*

'Is it true?' Bella demanded.

'What?' he demanded, wanting only to get back to Sarah. 'What is this?'

'It says that Mamma was not her father's child. That Nonna had an English lover in the war, that she seduced grandpa so that he would think her baby was his and marry her. She even named Mamma Alessandra. After him.'

Matteo did not want to soil his hands with this filth, but he had to know and he opened it, let his eyes skim over the words, the photographs.

'It says that this Englishwoman, Sarah, is my cousin. That you and I are nothing...'

It was all there. There was a photograph of Sarah's grandfather, Alexander—Lex—Randall. His war record. His medals. There was even a facsimile of a report in the *Maybridge Chronicle* dated June nineteen forty-four of his return home to his young wife and baby son months after he'd been given up for dead.

There were copies of Nonna's wedding certificate and his Aunt Alessandra's birth certificate, the dates telling their own story. Much was made of the fact that the child had been named for the lover rather than her grandmother.

All the little details that Sarah had told him that first evening about how the beautiful Lucia had saved her great-grandfather were there. The months they'd spent together, hidden from everyone in the ruins of the house. How they'd eaten wild asparagus. Found a bottle of wine in the cellars of the villa that had been missed by the soldiers who had destroyed the house. Things that only she could have known.

And there was a photograph of Rosa Lucia Leone—Nonna, seventeen or eighteen years old. Stunningly beautiful, the image of Bella, sitting on the wall where he'd found Sarah. Her heart in her eyes.

The only thing they had wrong was her name. She was Rosa. No one had ever called her anything but that. Except, it seemed, her English lover.

But then she had been his light in the darkness. As Sarah had been his.

'Does Nonna know about this?' he asked.

Bella shook her head.

'Call Graziella. Make sure she doesn't see it, doesn't speak to anyone until I talk to her first.'

'It is true?' Bella demanded, anguish in every line of her beautiful face.

He looked again at the photograph of the young Alexander Randall, posed in his uniform after some medal ceremony. Sarah had his eyes. Held her head in just that way.

'Yes.'

Nonna had seen Sarah, recognised her. Gone away when he'd announced he was bringing her to stay for the weekend.

Hoping, no doubt, that it was a nine-day wonder. That he would swiftly tire of her...

'Poor Mamma.' Then, with a flash of her old fire, 'She did this? Sarah?'

He stood there, recalling every moment. His first sight of her. That first kiss. His certainty that she was hiding something.

He had been warned. All his instincts had

told him that she was trouble but he hadn't
wanted to believe it. Hadn't wanted to believe
anything that Katerina told him.

'No,' he said. 'I did.'

Sarah opened the door wearing only a bathrobe,
hair a damp tangle about her face. A smile like
warm honey that went straight to his heart, he
didn't want to believe it.

'Matteo…'

A voice that went straight to his groin.

He ignored the cues to forget everything he
knew, take her one more time—be alive just
one more time.

Her smile faltered as he stepped past her,
tossed the magazine on the coffee table, summoned up the steel before he turned to face her.

'Job done, Sarah. I don't imagine you plan
on hanging around, but if you have any ideas of
remaining in Rome I suggest you revise them.'

She was staring at him as if she didn't know
what he was talking about.

'I'm sure it's well within your repertoire to
create a family crisis requiring your immediate
return to England.'

'What?' she gasped.

'If you are still in Rome on Monday I will
see that you never get another job in teaching.
Anywhere in the world. That is a promise.'

She didn't say anything. She turned to the

magazine, picked it up, looked at the cover for a moment, then opened it. She couldn't understand the words, but the photographs spoke for themselves.

For a moment he thought she was going to say something, make some excuse, some justification.

Instead, she lifted her head and looked at him. Straight into his eyes, his heart and said, 'I'm sorry.'

Sarah didn't move for a long time after Matteo turned and walked out of her apartment, quietly closing the door behind him.

Then she found the memory stick that Pippa had given her and looked at all the documents Federico had in a file named 'Serrone'.

Most of it was in Italian, but there were emails from England from newspaper archives, documents they'd sent him about Lex. The birth and marriage certificates that had been reproduced in the magazine. Typed notes that she had enough Italian to understand were transcripts from the conversation they'd had over supper. Clearly he'd been recording her.

There was even her photograph of Lucia that he must have downloaded from her netbook when he was pretending to help her.

There was enough evidence to prove that she was innocent of the ultimate betrayal, but it hardly mattered. She might not have fired the bullet, but she had loaded the gun.

She was responsible.

She picked up the phone, made a call to the Headmaster, explaining that a family crisis meant that she was required at home. That no, she didn't foresee any chance of her returning.

Then she called Pippa. She didn't answer, but it didn't matter. She only wanted to leave a message telling her that Federico hadn't been having an affair. And that since his secret meetings meant that he could probably afford a new laptop, he would no doubt forgive her for wrecking his old one.

She spent the rest of the day cleaning the flat, emptying the cupboards, packing her bags. On Monday she handed her keys, along with a box of groceries, to Signora Priverno, called a taxi and, carrying her lemon thyme under her arm, dragged her suitcase back down the hill.

Nonna, having looked at the magazine, summoned the entire family to the villa to tell them her story. How she'd found her airman, fallen in love. That when the Conte returned, badly wounded from the war, she had nursed him. How, when he realised that she was pregnant, he had married her.

'I was a mother for his son,' she said. 'And his injuries were such that he could have no more children of his own.' She took her daughter's hand. 'He could not have loved you more if you had been his own. You were, he said, his gift from God.' She turned to Matteo. 'Where is Sarah? It is time I met her.'

'She has gone home.'

'You sent her away?'

'She betrayed him, Nonna,' Bella declared. 'Betrayed us all.'

'For what purpose, Matteo?' Nonna asked. 'A part in a film?'

'No…' The idea was clearly ridiculous.

'Money?'

Money… It had to be that and yet it was hard to reconcile with the woman who had come to Isola del Serrone, lit a candle for Lucia Mancini. Prayed for her soul even though she knew she was not Lex's lover.

'Does it matter why she did it?' he said.

'What did she say to you when you confronted her?'

He'd forgotten how relentless Nonna could be and he caught a glimpse of the steel it must have taken to rescue Alexander Randall. Hide him for months. Keep him warm, fed. To keep her secret for a lifetime. Not just for her husband, but her daughter, her granddaughter. For Randall himself.

'She said… "I'm sorry".'

No attempt at excuses. No justification. None of Katerina's pleading for him to understand.

He couldn't get the sound of it out of his head.

Couldn't erase the look on her face. As if someone had taken away her life.

It was Alessandra who spoke next. 'This man, Alexander Randall. He is my father. Bella's grandfather. Can we meet him?'

'Matteo will go to England and invite him to return to Isola del Serrone. Meet a family he never knew existed,' Nonna said.

'No.'

She did not argue but instead got to her feet.

'Nonna. Where are you going?'

'Alexander built the first hives here for me. His bees will want to know that he is alive.'

'Matteo...' His aunt was looking at him. They were all looking at him.

'No!'

'Please.'

'If you want to see him, then go and find him.' He gestured at the magazine. 'I'm sure if you offer them the chance to take photographs of the family reunion, they'll fly you there first class. But leave me out of it.'

ITALIAN FOR BEGINNERS

There is a song that begins something like, 'Thanks for the memories'.

*That's all I asked of you, Matteo—
memories—and you delivered. I will
carry always the memory of you on the
path where Lex and Lucia said goodbye.
Where we said hello. We were very good
at hello...*

*I will carry the memory of tossing
a coin, warm from your hand, into the
Trevi, saying goodbye to my old life. You
gave me the courage to do that.*

*I will treasure the memory of your face
in the candlelight in the courtyard of your
home, in the moonlight as we made the
sweetest love, in the sunlight as we cut
grapes together.*

*I will treasure the nights we shared, the
days, the laughter. Your precious trust.*

*I wanted to give you that, too. Memo-
ries to cherish. To bring a smile to your
face one day years from now as you cut
the first grapes and remember an Englishwoman who passed through your life.
Shared a few of the stops on the journey.*

*Memories to make you ache a little
when you lie awake in the moonlight remembering a long ago love not with sadness, but with pleasure.*

*Instead you will only remember me as
another woman who betrayed you.*

Lex warned me not to stir up the past

and if I had listened to him, stayed away from Isola del Serrone, hadn't talked to Pippa, your family would not have been exposed so brutally.

I knew, of course I knew, that your Nonna was Lucia the moment I set eyes on Bella, but I said nothing because it was Lucia's secret and if I had been fortunate to meet her, I would have talked to her, told her about Lex, the life he had, we all had, thanks to her, but I would never have betrayed her secret.

All I ever wanted to know was that she was safe. That she was well cared for. To help, if she was not. Our family owed her that because without her courage, her love, my grandmother would not have been born. Nor my mother. And there would have been no Sarah Gratton.

Maybe you think that would be no bad thing, Matteo, and I cannot blame you for that. But I wouldn't have missed a moment of knowing you, carissimo.

Grazie milione *for the memories,* Matteo.

The Italian was rubbish, but she was just a beginner and her books were packed in the bottom of her suitcase. The meaning, she hoped, was clear enough.

'Siete la mia aria...' Sarah whispered as her flight was called. 'You are my air.'

She hit 'publish', knowing that Matteo would never read it. But it was a comfort to know that the words were out there, somewhere in cyber-space.

Motive... The word nagged at him. What possible motive would have driven anyone to expose his family in such a way?

Money, fame, revenge.

It had to be money. Nothing else made sense.

He prowled the empty palazzo, unable to sleep, drawn inexorably to his office, his laptop. The one remaining connection. Her blog. Would it still be there? Or would she have deleted it, as he'd attempted to delete her from his life.

He clicked on the bookmark. Dreading what might be there, what truth she might have revealed. But he had to know. He started to read.

Betrayed.

The word mocked him. Was it possible to hear the sound of a heart breaking?

Sarah had not betrayed him, he had betrayed her. Her truth, her love.

Self-obsessed to the point of paranoia, he had been judge, jury and executioner. The accused given no chance to defend herself.

If he'd needed a whip to beat himself with,

her friend Pippa told him exactly what had happened when he contacted her. That her boyfriend, working in the press office of a government ministry, had used his press contacts to sell a story that he'd stumbled on. Used Sarah, who'd had no idea that his family was involved with her Lucia.

'Rome wasn't to your taste?' Lex asked.

'I loved it.'

'But you didn't stay.'

'No. I messed up so badly, Lex. I was stupid, thoughtless. I hardly know how to tell you what I've done.'

'Parla come magni,' he said.

Speak as you eat. It was an expression she'd known since she was a little girl.

As a child she hadn't even realised it wasn't English. It was simply what he said when she had something difficult to get off her chest.

When she was older, she'd assumed it was Latin. It was only when she'd heard people use it in Rome that she understood that it was something he must have learned during those hard months in Italy with Lucia.

She kept it simple, beginning with the moment she'd decided to go to Isola del Serrone and not stopping until Matteo had arrived with the magazine.

Then she showed him the magazine that

Matteo had tossed onto her table. The photographs of his love, a daughter he'd never known. His lovely granddaughter.

By the end of her story they were both weeping and she reached into her pocket for Matteo's handkerchief, dried his tears, dried her own.

'She is well? Lucia.'

'Rosa Lucia.'

'Lucia to me. She was out searching for a stray sheep. I saw her light. Heard her calling.'

'She is a contessa, Lex. A widow for many years, but well, active and, as you can see, Isabella is just like her. So lovely. Everyone adores her.' She told him what Angelo had said. Told him about the opera. About the moment when she'd realised the connection. 'I wasn't going to say anything. Not to Bella. Not to Matteo.'

'You did nothing wrong, Sarah.'

'You told me to leave well alone. I should have listened.'

'I'm glad that you didn't.' He leaned forward and kissed her head. 'Go and tell the bees your story.'

She knew he wanted to be on his own with his memories, to look at the photographs of his daughter and granddaughter and she left him to it. The garden was chilly after Italy, but not for a November afternoon.

The sun was out, there were plenty of flowers and the bees were still making sorties into the garden.

'Well, guys. You didn't expect to see me again so soon. Lex will be down for a chat soon, I expect, to tell you all the news. That we have family we never knew about.' They hummed quietly, going about their business. 'As for me, well, I found someone, too. Just what the doctor ordered, in fact. Someone to make memories with. Someone I could have spent a lifetime making memories with.'

Matteo heard Sarah before he saw her.

'The thing is, I didn't mean to fall in love. That just wasn't supposed to happen. I was in love with Tom, or at least still clinging to the notion that I was in love with him. I realise now that I'd already outgrown him but just wasn't prepared to admit it. I had my entire life planned out. The house, the wedding, the dress, even the children. Two boys for Tom and a girl for me. To let go of that I needed to hit a bump in the road. Or maybe a rock.'

She was sitting sideways on a small bench, her legs up, her arms around them, her head resting on her knees, chatting away to the bees.

'Tom ran into Louise. I hit Matteo. A head-on collision. It was as if someone had turned the lights on. Like watching *The Wizard of Oz* when it turns from black and white to Technicolor, and here's my problem.' She swung her legs down, leaned forward, elbows on knees. 'If I hadn't been searching for Lucia I would never have met…'

Much as he just wanted to stand there and listen to her, it was like eavesdropping on a conversation with God, and he stepped forward.

She straightened up, looked at him, and for a heartbeat it was all there, in her face. Everything she was feeling. Everything he was feeling. Pain, joy, love. It was as if the world had paused, holding its breath, or maybe it was just him because, after a moment, she shifted over to make room beside her and continued talking.

'If I hadn't been searching for Lucia, I would never have met Matteo. Which would have meant I had no memories. And Lex wouldn't know that his Lucia is alive and well, or that he had a daughter, a granddaughter. Try as hard as I might, I can't regret that.'

She turned back to the bees.

'That was really something. Coming face to face with Bella. I wanted to tell Matteo then, but I couldn't, because it was Lucia's secret.' She paused. 'Are you following this, bees?'

'I don't know about the bees, but you've got my total attention.'

She looked back at him. 'How did you find me?'

'I talked to Pippa. She had your address in her files.'

'She could get the sack for that,' she commented.

'Do you think she would have cared? Once she knew what she'd done? I talked to your Headmaster, too. He's expecting you back at work next Monday.'

She was staring at him. He couldn't bear it...

'Will they listen to me, do you think?' he asked. 'These foreign bees.'

'I don't see why not. As long as you stick to English. Try it.'

He sat for a while. 'I don't know where to begin.'

'Parla come magni, caro.'

Despite everything, that prompted a smile. 'You are full of surprises, *cara*.' Then, turning to the bees, 'Okay. Here it is. I didn't mean to fall in love. It wasn't supposed to happen. I met this woman and, despite the fact that night became day when I kissed her, I told myself that I could control it. That no one could touch me because I'd been burned so badly that there was nothing left but hard scar tissue. To feel... To trust...' He leaned forward just as she had. 'How can I tell you what it's like to lose that? To find it again... Except you don't. The minute there's the slightest doubt it's gone, you lash out because the pain is unbearable and then you realise you're wrong, but there's nothing you can do or say that will ever put that right.'

A bee settled on his sleeve.

'They're listening,' Sarah said.

'Will they hear me if I tell you how sorry I am?' he said huskily.

'They heard me. And I am sorry. I betrayed you and I betrayed Lucia.'

'No… You asked for help from your friend.'

'It wasn't Pippa.'

'No. Her boyfriend, Federico Priverno, is a Press Officer in a government department these days, but you weren't to know that he was once a journalist. Not even Pippa knew that.' She shook her head. 'And you're right, if this hadn't happened, Lex wouldn't know he had another family. If this hadn't happened, Alessandra and Bella wouldn't know they had a father, a grandfather.'

He continued, 'Nonna never doubted you. She wanted me to come and bring you home. Bring you both home. And your parents, too, if they would like to come.'

'And you?'

'Lex and your parents are welcome, but the only person I care about here is you.' He took her hand, lifted it to his lips. '*Siete la mia aria, carissima.* Will you forgive me? Come home with me. Trust me with your life as I trust you with mine? Take the journey with me. A thousand stops, ports, harbours.'

'You've forgotten the desert island.'

'Not for a minute. I have one picked out for our honeymoon. I love you, Sarah.' The bee flew away and he took her into his arms. 'I want your face to be the first thing I see every morning. The last thing I see every night. To still be making memories together sixty years from now.'

ITALIAN FOR BEGINNERS

An Italian wedding is an amazing thing. The entire village is decorated with flowers and bunting. The square filled with tables, a small orchestra set up on a dais. Unlike weddings in the UK, the guests don't arrive and sit quietly in the pews. They wander about, chatting and laughing and then, when the bride arrives at the church, they line up and applaud her as she joins her groom.

There is dancing and food—I cannot begin to describe the food—and the fountain in the square does not run with water, but with Serrone wine.

And that was just for my great-grandfather and my Matteo's Nonna—his step-great-grandmother.

No. Just kidding. We married on the same day, a double celebration, and since a photograph is worth a thousand words, here are pictures to keep you entertained for the rest of the school year.

As for me, it's farewell to Italian for Beginners. I'm now a fully-fledged Italian Contessa—so you'd better practise your curtsey for the next time I visit Maybridge. Until then,

Un milione di baci! *(That's love and kisses.)*

* * * * *

A sneaky peek at next month...

RIVA™

LIVE LIFE TO THE FULL – GIVE IN TO TEMPTATION

My wish list for next month's titles...

In stores from 6th January 2012:

❏ First Time Lucky? – Natalie Anderson

❏ Runaway Bride – Barbara Hannay

❏ We'll Always Have Paris – Jessica Hart

Available at WHSmith, Tesco, Asda, Eason, Amazon and Apple

Just can't wait?

Visit us Online

You can buy our books online a month before they hit the shops! **www.millsandboon.co.uk**

1211/0

MILLS & BOON Book Club *Save up to £35*

Join the Mills & Boon Book Club

Subscribe to **Riva**™ today for
12 or 6 months and you could
save up to £35!

We'll also treat you to these fabulous extras:

- 🌹 **FREE L'Occitane gift set
  worth £10**

- 🌹 **FREE home delivery**

- 🌹 **Books up to 2 months
  ahead of the shops**

- 🌹 **Bonus books, exclusive offers…
  and much more!**

Subscribe now at
www.millsandboon.co.uk/subscribeme

**Visit us
Online**

Save up to £35 – find out more at
www.millsandboon.co.uk/subscribeme

SUBS/OFFER/R

Book of the Month

MILLS & BOON

LUCY ELLIS
Untouched by His Diamonds

We love this book because...

Step into the glam, witty and scorchingly intense world of Lucy Ellis... She'll sweep you away with her contemporary spin on the alpha male—they don't get sexier than her delectable Russian hero, Serge Marinov!

On sale 16th December

Visit us Online

Find out more at
www.millsandboon.co.uk/BOTM

1211/BOTM

Have Your Say

You've just finished your book.
So what did you think?

We'd love to hear your thoughts on our
'Have your say' online panel
www.millsandboon.co.uk/haveyoursay

- Easy to use
- Short questionnaire
- Chance to win Mills & Boon® goodies

Visit us Online

Tell us what you thought of this book now at
www.millsandboon.co.uk/haveyoursay

YOUR_SAY

Special Offers

Every month we put together collections and longer reads written by your favourite authors.

Here are some of next month's highlights— and don't miss our fabulous discount online!

On sale 16th December   On sale 16th December   On sale 6th January

Find out more at
www.millsandboon.co.uk/specialreleases

Visit us Online

0112/ST/MB35